Ria Montori is no stranger to kicking ass. Despite her petite size, she's a former Sandarian military officer currently serving the Cavacent clan and adjusting to life on a strange planet called Earth. She has no time to search for her psi-mate, the one being who could bring her pleasure beyond any mere physical intimacy. Which doesn't explain why she's bonding with a Curzan native who just killed a government official.

Ty Sordina hates Ria's kind. The Sandarians enslaved his people and murdered his parents in front him when he was a child. He has sought revenge ever since, and nothing will get in his way. Especially not a feisty redhead who challenges his every instinct and calls to his psi like no other. But there is a war coming. And the two beings who want nothing to do with each other hold the fate of an entire planet in the heat of their undeniable desire . . .

Books by Sabine Priestley

Alien Attachments Series
Alien Attachments
Rebellion

Published by Kensington Publishing Corporation

Rebellion

Alien Attachments

Sabine Priestley

LYRICAL PRESS
Kensington Publishing Corp.
www.kensingtonbooks.com

LYRICAL PRESS BOOKS are published by
Kensington Publishing Corp.
119 West 40th Street
New York, NY 10018

All Kensington titles, imprints, and distributed lines are available at special quantity discounts for bulk purchases for sales promotion, premiums, fund-raising, educational, or institutional use.

Special book excerpts or customized printings can also be created to fit specific needs. For details, write or phone the office of the Kensington Sales Manager: Kensington Publishing Corp., 119 West 40th Street, New York, NY 10018. Attn. Sales Department. Phone: 1-800-221-2647.

Lyrical Press and Lyrical Press logo Reg. U.S. Pat. & TM Off.

First Electronic Edition: October 2015
eISBN-13: 978-1-61650-579-0
eISBN-10: 1-61650-579-6

First Print Edition: October 2015
ISBN-13: 978-1-61650-597-4
ISBN-10: 1-61650-597-4

Printed in the United States of America

To my awesome family for putting up with my craziness. A huge thanks to Renee Rocco at Lyrical Press for taking a chance on me. To my amazing Lyrical editor Corinne DeMaagd, you are the voice in my head. Finally, to my great friend and totally awesome editor, Victoria Baksa, you rock!

Chapter 1

Ria Montori leaned against the transparent panel with arms crossed, enjoying the view of Earth below. It was good to get off-planet, if only to the Cavacents' cloaked base station. The little blue planet hung suspended in space, so different from the purples and greens of Sandaria.

Times like these gave her a chance to reflect. She was proud of what she'd accomplished. Because of her small size, she'd had to work twice as hard as anyone else to be taken seriously. Graduating second in her class in the military academy had helped. After her obligatory three years of service, she'd signed on with the Cavacent clan and now had a coveted spot as an Earth Protector, EP for short. But things were changing in the Sandarian Empire, and her world along with it.

She and Dani Standich, the newest member of the EP team, were overseeing the arrival of supplies from Sandaria. EPs had a wide range of duties outside of protecting Earth. The Cavacent clan had escaped Sandaria during the fall of the old empire in such a hurry, many things had been left behind. Due to the animosity of both the new planetary ruler and the Portal Masters' Guild, they might never be able to return, but with the help of those still living there, things were working out. They had been able to recover a large percentage of belongings they'd been forced to leave behind, and most of Rucon Cavacent's shipping business had survived intact.

"You okay?" Dani asked. "You look sad."

Ria regarded the tall blonde. She was a stark contrast to her own petite build and fiery red hair. Where Ria's world had shrunk, Dani's had exploded—other worlds, aliens, empires, all laid bare to her. She blew out a breath. "I'm okay. Glad we pulled this duty today. I don't know if this will make sense to you, but I'm feeling a little claustrophobic on Earth."

"How can you be claustrophobic on a planet?" Dani asked.

She tried to find the words to explain. "Because Sandaria is home to the Portal Masters, it's probably the most connected planet in the galaxy. You could request travel to at least a dozen planets. Starships are constantly coming and going." Both women wore the standard EP attire of black button-up shirt, black jeans, and boots. Ria turned to face Dani and shoved her hands in her front pockets. "I spent three years cruising the stars in the military before I hired on with the Cavacents. And now, with the fall of the emperor, that little ball out there is all there is. Does that make sense?"

Dani squeezed her arm. "It does. I mean, it's kind of weird for someone like me who never knew anything but Earth, but it makes sense." Dani bounced up and down on her toes. "I still get goose bumps being able to see Earth from out here. Don't you?"

Ria gave her a smirk. Her friend radiated a disgusting amount of happy. She'd recently bonded with Ria's boss, Ian Cavacent, and there were times Ria wanted to smack the happy out of her. She was glad for them, of course, but one could only take so much sunshine.

It was a calm day below, with few clouds to hide the surface.

"I still can't believe it," Ria said, tucking a strand of hair behind her ear. "A few months ago Earth was just a job. Now it's home."

Dani huffed. "A few months ago, I didn't know aliens existed or that I had super powers."

Ria smacked Dani on the elbow. "Psi isn't super powers."

Dani gave her a look.

"Yeah, okay. From a human perspective, maybe it is," Ria said. "We're Supergirls."

Ria's com started screaming like a teenager, making both women jump. Dani's com followed a moment later with the atmosphere breach alert.

Ria wasn't sure what surprised her more, the screaming or the breach. "Harvey, silence the alert," Ria said. "And stop screaming." She'd modified her com on Earth, giving it access to the Internet. Over time and with some tweaking on her part, it was developing a personality. The results so far had proved amusing. She never knew what Harvey would do.

"Yes, ma'am," her com said, sounding miffed.

Dani shot her a what-the-fuck look as they bolted for the portal. "That scared the crap out of me."

"Sorry." Ria stifled a laugh. "I've been playing with the interface. Screaming female wasn't exactly what I was going for."

Ria pulled up the status of the six cloaked transport ships that currently surrounded Earth. Two of them were picking up an alien signature on the planet. *How is that even possible?* They stepped through the portal together. Ria felt the familiar pull on her body and tingle of her psi as they were transported from the station to Earth. They emerged in Ian and Dani's study on Cat Island in the Bahamas. The portal exited through the fireplace and onto woven grass rugs. White floor-to-ceiling bookcases covered the walls, and a massive desk sat near a window overlooking the cliff and water below.

"What gives, Ian?" Ria said. "How could we have an atmosphere breach without an approach from space?"

Ian ran a hand through his wavy blond hair. It was obvious that he and Dani were communicating telepathically via their bond.

Dani's face paled.

"Your ships picked up alien signatures on the planet," Ria said. "Who is it, and how did they get here?"

The shock was evident in Ian's voice. "They exited hyper-space inside the impact zone."

"Frack me," Ria said as the meaning sunk in. *Who would do that?* Inside the zone meant it was pure luck they didn't exit partially or fully inside the planet. Earth could have been destroyed today. A cold sweat formed on her skin as the horrific scene played out in her mind.

The fourth EP currently on Earth at the moment entered the room from the hallway. The arrogant albino, Armond, had arrived from the tunnels and looked as shocked as the rest of them.

The final EP, Marco, was on a mission with Ian's uncle and wouldn't be back for a few weeks, at least.

Ian projected the status holo and searched the incoming data.

Armond joined them as information updates came in on the vid. "Identified?"

"Torogs," Ian said, looking puzzled.

"Where are they headed?" Ria asked.

Ian scratched his head. "They were headed straight toward Asia, but they've changed course."

Ria followed the trajectory of the signal. "They're coming here." It was impossible not to remember the last time the Torogs had visited Cat Island. They'd stormed the villa. Their ball-jointed limbs and leathery bodies had half climbed, half fallen through the dining room window. At the same time, they'd smashed in the front door. They'd managed to slice off Marco's hand before he and everyone but Dani and Ian had made it through the portal back to Sandaria. Those two had almost died when the Torogs bombed the tunnel that led from Ian's villa. They'd barely survived by pulling off a nearly impossible portal move and following the others to his home planet. The whole thing had been a mess. "Is this some kind of joke?"

"No joke," Ian said. He brought up the villa's sensors that showed it cloaked and shielded. "They can't get in here. Question is, what do they want? Why did they change course?"

"What if they weren't headed to Asia, but the Maldives?" Ria asked.

The EPs had bases around the globe. Ian on Cat Island, Ria in Lago Como, Marco in New Zealand, and Armond in the Maldives.

Ian raised an eyebrow. "Go on."

"It would explain the change of course if they're tracking Armond. They were headed to his base. Now they're coming here."

"Why would they be doing that?" Armond looked down on her with an air of superiority.

"I don't know. You're the self-proclaimed genius. You figure it out."

They all watched as the Torog signal approached the Island. It hovered around the Cat for nearly ten minutes before blasting out of the atmosphere and setting off another round of alarms. They followed the signature until they were satisfied the aliens weren't coming back.

Ian's com signaled an incoming call. He spoke briefly and disconnected. "My father wants to see us."

A network of subterranean tunnels interconnected by portals existed deep under the Earth's surface. The EPs used them to travel the globe and the Cavacent clan for mining the rare and precious mineral carnium. The trace mineral was a required element in the fuel used by their Faster Than Light, or FTL, interstellar ships. The team filed out of Ian's library and headed for the cruiser. Twenty minutes later, they were gathered in Ria's villa in Bellagio, Italy. Rucon Cavacent, Ian's father, had chosen Lago Como as the location of the new Cavacent compound, currently under construction in the hills above the lake. In the meantime, Ria's villa was the most centrally located and served as temporary headquarters. They gathered around the large dining room table. Ria had instantly felt at home the first time she had seen the marble floors and rich browns and reds of the walls of the ornate Italian villa. She'd inherited it from a previous EP and wouldn't change a thing.

Rucon was not happy as he wrapped up a call to someone on his com. "They must pay for this. They could have destroyed us. Not to mention the entire planet is buzzing with the news of something leaving the atmosphere. Earth is still a dark planet. They don't know about us." Rucon paused, listening before he continued. "Agreed. Thank you, Torril. I'll be in touch."

Torril Anantha. Ria was impressed. Not many people were on a first name basis with the head of the newly formed Galactic Trade Organization.

Rucon tapped his fingers on the tabletop. "He's launching an investigation. Even with the current state of unrest, risking an entire planet warrants the GTO's attention. There will also be a small battleship stationed along with our transport ships. If they attempt this again, we'll be able to hunt them down."

Chasing the Torogs wasn't an option with the transport ships. Although heavily armed, they weren't designed for pursuit.

"For now," Rucon said standing, "we keep all bases shielded at all times."

Rucon was taking this seriously. Full-time shielding meant full-time monitoring as well. The shields prevented anyone and anything from crossing their perimeter. From the local deliveryman to birds and animals. It wouldn't do to have humans walking into an invisible wall.

Rucon interrupted her thoughts before she could ask how long he expected to keep the shields active. "One more thing. Assuming everything remains quiet, Mara and I have accepted an invitation to attend the Summer's Ball on Mitah this year. An old friend of mine lives there." He scanned the faces around the table. "We've all been working hard since coming to Earth. I think it's time for a break. As long as we don't have further complications from the Torogs, I'm extending the invitation to the whole team. We'll make a portal back to Earth as soon as we get to Mitah."

"Excellent," Ria said.

The others were equally excited about the prospect.

Rucon said his goodbyes, leaving the rest to discuss plans.

Dani, who'd never been anywhere other than Earth and Sandaria, was bouncing up and down. "Anyone been to Mitah?"

"I've never been," Ria said, "but I dated a guy from there for a while at the academy. It's supposed to be beautiful." And it would be great to have another world to go to occasionally.

"And you guys?" Dani asked.

Armond shook his head, but Ian nodded. "We've been to the ball a few times. You're going to love it. It's a three-day visual spectacle, complete with a masquerade ball. You two"—Ian nodded to Ria and Dani—"are going to need to go ahead of time for dresses."

Dani clapped her hands like a child.

Ria nearly choked on her water. "Why? We're an hour and a half from Milan. World class designers and all that."

Ian crossed his arms and smiled. "Yes, but you can only get Mitan silk from Mitah, and trust me. You want Mitan silk."

* * * *

It had been four days since the Torog's return to Earth. There had been no further attempts. Whether that was due to the battleship now orbiting with Rucon's transport ships or not, they had no idea. Ria and the other EPs were forty minutes into a training session in her sim room on Bellagio. They'd chosen a tropical jungle with four different types of alien life forms for variety. Distinguishing between harmless native wildlife and deadly aliens wasn't always easy. It was a team mission, and so far, they hadn't lost anyone. Today's weapon of choice was a small handheld laser called a dart. It worked like a gun on one setting and like a two-and-a-half-foot sword in the other. The training models were designed to deplete rapidly over time until only the sword function remained, and that got shorter until only the casing was left. So far, everyone still had functioning guns.

It was she and Dani's turn to hold their base. Ian and Armond flushed the surrounding area. Ian was ahead in kills, but so far, she and Dani were ahead on team saves. So as usual, the women were keeping them alive, and the guys were shooting things.

Ria wiped the sweat from her eyes. "We need to pick a desert next time. This humidity sucks."

"You get used to it," Dani said.

The bushes to their left rustled, and both women swung their lasers in the ready.

Ian stepped out, and Ria sparked with envy when he grabbed Dani and planted a kiss on her before he disappeared back into the foliage.

"Seriously?" Ria said. "You can't go an hour without locking lips?"

Ian's laughter rippled through the trees.

Dani beamed.

Ria rolled her eyes.

Another rustle, and a four-legged creature with razor sharp teeth launched itself at Ria's chest. "Morits!" Ria called out as she sliced the critter in half.

The sound of Ian and Armond battling away let her know they'd found the nasty critters as well. Six more made it past the men. Dani made easy work of the two that had targeted her. Ria nearly made it unscathed but when four hit her at once from all sides, one managed to latch onto her lower arm. Those jaws had some serious force, and her hand popped off, dropping the creature to the ground with it.

"Aw, come on. Not fair. There were four of them." Ria lifted up her wrist and studied the bloody stump. "Halt sim."

Ian and Armond approached from opposite ends of the clearing, equally covered in sweat.

Dani came to her side and inspected her handless arm. "It would almost be easier if they were bigger. It's hard to keep track of them when they're so small."

"Perhaps your relative height to the ground also contributed to your demise," Armond said.

Ria glared at him. "Are you *seriously* going there?"

"I'm simply stating that you were closer to them than Dani."

"Whatever," Ria said. "Little shits. Reset sim," she called out.

Morit bodies and Ria's hand evaporated. The illusion of a bloody stump did, as well, and her own hand reappeared as they all caught their breath. The jungle around them melted into the floor, and they soon stood in the metal gray of the sim room.

"That wasn't bad," Ian said. "We made it nearly an hour, outnumbered five to one. I'm good with that."

Ria was annoyed by the fact that she'd been the one to go out first. She had a competitive nature and hated losing.

She was still in a bad mood later that night when she sat at the kitchen table with her two Support Agents, Gina and Battista. They lived in a suite of rooms off the kitchen. Together, they cooked, cleaned, and took care of the estate. They looked like a normal, older Italian couple—a bit on the pudgy side, but sprightly enough. In truth, they were both highly trained and fully in the know about aliens. Across the table, they were giggling over a shared joke. Looking at them fawn over each other, you'd think they were psi-mates like Dani and Ian, but they weren't. They were simply humans in love and, at the moment, irritating.

Gina finished a bite of pasta and chuckled at Ria. "Ms. Dani, she tell me you lose today. It's not like you to lose, no?"

Ria bit the side of her cheek, still steaming. "I was being attacked by four furballs with teeth. One of them took my hand off." She shoved a large forkful into her mouth.

Apparently sensing Ria's chagrin, Battista jumped into the conversation. "We ran into the Mancini boy in town yesterday. He said to tell you hello and give him a call someday."

"He likes you, all right." Gina patted her arm. "You should call him. Maybe have dinner."

Ria pulled a strand of hair from her pasta. "If he ever decides to grow up, maybe I will."

Battista burst out laughing. "If he's like his *papi,* that will never happen."

"How about that cook in town?" Gina said. "He always makes a point of coming out and saying hello when you go to his restaurant."

Ria appreciated their concern, but the conversation just made everything worse. She pushed her chair back and grabbed her plate.

"*Bellisima*, where are you going?" Battista asked.

"*Si,*" Gina said, frowning at the food left on her plate. "You have not finished. You don't like it? I can make you something else." Gina moved to get up, as well, but Ria waved her back down.

"No, no. I'm just not hungry right now." She wasn't usually this abrupt, but between spending the afternoon around Dani and Ian and now these two, her single status was starting to annoy her. She thought about walking into town and having a drink but didn't think that would help. With the clan's move to Earth, the constant construction of the compound, and flipping Torogs showing up, dating hadn't been a priority.

At least now, she had something to look forward to. The Summer's Ball sounded like the perfect excursion. "I'll save the rest for later. You two enjoy dinner. I'm going to hit the sim room for awhile before I call it a night." Normally, she wouldn't want a workout this late, but she was feeling antsy. Her psi buzzed with too much energy. In lieu of having a decent male specimen in her life, a match or two in the sim room would have to do.

Chapter 2

"It's only four days. I think you'll live." Leaning over, Ria flipped on the tracking beacon for the tower on Mitah's landing port.

"You could at least show a little sympathy," Dani said from the seat next to her.

"Are all humans this sappy when they find their mate?"

"I'm afraid we have a long and sordid history of embarrassing acts and misdeeds, all committed in the name of love." She kissed Ian's image on her com screen.

"Ugh. Get a grip. We only have two days to find three days worth of party clothes down there. I need you focused, not pining over Ian."

The cockpit display window framed the planet as it grew larger with their approach. Mitah was a double-mooned planet in a single star system very similar to Earth. They would return in a little over a month for the Summer's Ball.

"So, you gonna pick out Ian's outfits?" Ria asked.

"He didn't want anything new. Just a mask for the masquerade ball on the second night. Apparently, there's not a lot of call for luminescent suits, other than during the ball." Dani reached for her com, stopped herself, and started tapping her fingers on her knee. "You'd think you could get the material on other worlds."

"Only knock-offs. For the real thing, you have to go to Mitah. It's actually tourism genius if you ask me."

"I suppose."

The silkworms on Mitah produced bioluminescent thread. The fabric was unnaturally strong, lightweight, and never faded. The government limited the amount tourists could buy and guarded the production secrets.

"From what I've heard," Ria said, "every attempt to smuggle the worms off-planet has ended with the poor critter's demise. So, we go to Mitah, get fitted, and everything's ready when we return."

Ria adjusted their descent to match the port guidance signal. "How's Ian doing with Armond?"

Armond and the rogue Portal Masters on Earth were trying to teach Ian how to make a portal using the device the EPs captured from the Torogs shortly before the fall of the empire.

"He thinks he's nearly there. It's a good thing, too, because he's really getting fed up with Armond's arrogance."

"Gods, I bet," Ria said.

"Ian said the other Portal Masters being there helps." Dani let out a small groan. "I'm next you know. Not looking forward to spending hours with Armond."

Ria laughed. "I know. Good luck with that. Still, if you and Ian can learn to make portals as well as Armond, we'll all feel a lot better."

"Yeah, having that condescending ass in charge of all our portals is seriously unnerving. I wonder if Mordo and Durgan are having any luck."

"Me, too. I don't think Rucon's heard any news yet."

Ian's uncle, Mordo, and a Portal Master named Durgan were searching distant worlds for others like Armond, Ian, and Dani, who possessed an alternate form of psi. Marco, their last EP, was with them for protection.

"Do you think they'll make it back in time for the ball?" Dani asked.

"Doubtful," Ria said. "It's a shame, really. Can you imagine Marco at the ball?"

Dani laughed. "He'd have women lined up in a row." She slipped her com out and pulled up a photo. "I miss Ian."

Ria sighed. Another hour and a half and they'd be on the surface. Hopefully, shopping would be a distraction. It was a day and a half from Earth to the interstellar jump point, and another two to Mitah's spaceport. They planned on two days to purchase their gowns, masks, and anything else they could find, and then it was back home until they returned for the ball itself.

"We'll get some shopping done, then we're having lunch with Laric Jara and his folks. Hopefully that will take your mind off Ian."

"I wouldn't bet on it," Dani said, sliding the com back into her pocket. "I do need to think about something else, though." She turned her gaze to the planet below. "What is that?"

A large object rose from the far side of Mitah. Ria smiled. "It's the second moon. I can't wait to get a look at them at night."

"Sweet," Dani said, resting her arms on the console. "Mitah's beautiful. Lots of water."

"It is pretty. Smaller than Earth and has only about three-quarters the amount of land."

Ria adjusted their course and took a moment to admire the vehicle. The Cavacent clan spared no expense on their fleet of transport ships. They brought to the vessels a level of opulence rarely seen in transports of this class. Even their terrestrial shuttles, like the one they were in now, were over the top. The best Sandarian leather and control panels inlaid with exotic woods gave the shuttle the feel of a luxury liner rather than a transport ship. "We'll be landing at the capital of Starfall on the southern continent of Mooriac." Ria pointed to the upper right of the planet. "Laric will meet us at the port and take us to Watersedge where we can do some shopping." She sang the last word and winked at Dani.

Ria had never been to Mitah before, but she'd heard a lot about it. "Laric used to tell me stories about the wild beasts that live in the Trillian forests. I forget what they're called, but people come from all over to hunt them. It's a dangerous sport with a couple of deaths every year. Never understood why someone would risk their life to hunt a wild animal."

"Doesn't appeal to me either," Dani said.

"Especially with all the sim technology these days. I actually like hunting, just not for real."

Dani flipped on the polarization as the sun came into view beyond the planet. "Tell me about Laric. What's he like?"

"He's good looking, taller than me—"

"Everyone is taller than you," Dani interrupted.

Ria smacked Dani in the head with her psi. "He's a redhead, too. We used to get teased mercilessly by our classmates. It never bothered him, though. That's one of the things that drew me to him in the first place. Nothing gets under his skin."

"What happened with you two? We're staying with his folks, so obviously you're still friends."

"I don't know. We flirted through the first year at the academy, dated through the second, avoided each other for the third, and got to be friends again the final year." Their assigned approach vector popped up on the console in front of her, and she accepted it.

"What broke you up?"

"I guess it was sort of a mutual acknowledgment that what we had, although nice, wasn't very exciting. Just wasn't any passion there for me. No thrill. When I told him at the beginning of the third year that I wanted a break, he didn't argue." Ria entered a sequence of commands with her psi, enabling a manual approach. "We missed each other's company that year. When we started hanging out again, it was good. Just friends. Been that way ever since. We touch base now and then. When Rucon announced our little vacation here, I called him. I'm glad he's on leave. It will be nice to see him again."

"Who knows," Dani said. "Maybe it will work out this time."

"He's full-time military. I'd only see him on leave. Besides, I want what every Sandarian wants, what you and Ian have. I want a psi-mate. We were together long enough to know that's not happening." Ria checked the course and pushed her chair back. She set her com on the console in front of her and projected a mirror. She brushed her straight red hair and pulled it into a ponytail.

"Primping already?" Dani asked, pulling out her own brush.

"I haven't seen him in years. A girl's got to look her best."

"It was nice of his folks to let us stay with them."

"It was. Always nice to save a few credits. Hotels here cost a small fortune." Ria finished up and took back full control of the shuttle, bringing it in for a perfect landing.

* * * *

Interstellar travel always had an edge of cold to it. Ria flung her arms over the back of the seat of the open top cruiser, closed her eyes, and let the sun do its thing. She and Dani were dressed in the standard EP attire, and she looked forward to changing into summer clothes as the sun warmed her. "This is fantastic." She'd been a little nervous about seeing Laric, but they'd fallen into their old camaraderie like slipping on a favorite pair of jeans.

"Glad we had a nice sunny day for your arrival. I ordered it just for you two," Laric said.

"We appreciate that." Ria inhaled deeply and took in the view. They wound their way around the edge of Starfall, then out into the country towards Watersedge. It was a beautiful ride. Laric peppered them with local history and tidbits. The forests and mountain ranges of Mitah were highly celebrated. Protected from development, beings came from across the galaxy to trek, climb, and explore the stunning terrain. And of course, there was the hunting. The road to Watersedge hugged the largest of these natural preserves. Only two small towns stood between Starfall and their destination, and they were both low-tech. Probably lower class Mitans and their Curzan slaves.

Still, Ria took in the towering mountains in the distance, *if you have to be poor, this is a pretty awesome place to do it.* She imagined that between the garden plots next to nearly every home and the hunting possibilities of the preserve, they probably lived fairly well.

The mountains were heavily forested. Vertical cliffs ran along the base of the range to the left. It looked as though some cosmic giant had sliced off the foot of the range. One of the moons crested the peak. It would soon be tailed by its smaller brother.

They made good time, and Laric dropped them off at one end of the market while he took care of some business of his own before lunch.

Ria checked the list of places he'd sent to her com for shopping. "Harvey, show me a map of the places Laric suggested."

"Yes, sugar. Y'all are real close to this here specialty gown shop." Harvey spoke in a female voice with a Texan drawl.

Ria snorted.

"Nice," Dani said.

The holo showed a picture of a shop front expanding in size. Ria moved the holo to one side and saw it was only four or five doors from where they stood.

"Looks good to me, shall we?"

Dani swept her arm out. "After you, sugar."

Twenty minutes later, Ria pushed aside the flimsy curtain of a dressing stall and spun in circles over to the mirror. She loved the way the bottom of the dress flared out when she twirled. Purple silk and lace hugged her diminutive frame and accentuated her breasts. She took a deep breath, taking in the smell of incense and fresh ocean air. There was an energy here that had her totally fired up.

The shopkeeper had dedicated a large portion of the back of the shop to dressing rooms. Six stalls radiated from a circular waiting area. Floor-to-ceiling mirrors stood between each stall. A large, framed open doorway led to the shop floor, leaving the space bright and airy. Upbeat music piped in from overhead made for a fun atmosphere.

A man's voice came from out front, and Ria's stomach did an odd flip-flop. The lady shopkeeper laughed at something he said. "You're far too sweet, Ty. Now, come here and let me show you."

The small woman led a dark-haired man to the doorway. "Don't mind us, dears. Just some repairs that need doing."

Dani swept out of her stall and twirled to Ria's side.

The shopkeeper reached out and showed the man where the doorframe had been split in half. "The girls were perfectly behaved. It's when the boys showed up that things got out of control." She shook her head and handed the broken frame segment to the man. "They broke the bench in the third stall over there, as well."

"Don't worry, Mrs. Tiddle, I'll have it all fixed in no time." The man smiled, then turned to Ria.

Long bangs hung over part of his face and nearly covered smoky gray eyes.

Ria caught her breath as her psi buzzed. It was a crazy buzz, like something from a dream half-remembered. The kind where you wake yourself laughing only to have the memory go up in a puff of smoke. The reason for laughing was gone, but it left you happy.

He grinned and returned to the front of the shop.

"Hello? Earth to Ria? Or, Mitah to Ria, whatever." Dani snapped fingers in front of her face.

Ria focused on her friend. "Sorry, what did you say?"

"I said, what do you think of this?" Dani wore a white gown that had black gems woven throughout in a beguiling pattern. The dress would shine with an ethereal light of its own in the dark.

"Spectacular," Ria said. She glanced over to the doorway where the man had been and wondered if he'd be back soon.

The shopkeeper hustled in then with an armful of glittery, sheer fabric. She set them down on a bench and held one up.

"Oh, they're beautiful," Dani said rushing over.

White wings made with loosely woven silk had a life of their own as Mrs. Tiddle held them up. "Turn around, dear."

Dani spun around, and the woman attached the wings to her back. The theme of the infamous Summer's Ball on Mitah this year was a mythical creature called the *Swali*. They were not unlike Earth's fairies and were said to have magical abilities, including seeing into the future.

The shopkeeper extended another set of wings, purple this time to match Ria's dress.

Ria fingered the delicate material. Silky soft, they sparkled with her touch. "I'm afraid I'll break them."

"Goodness no, sweetie. This is Mitan silk. It's been treated to be somewhat rigid, and is very strong. Now turn around."

The crazy energy was back, and Ria laughed as she spun around and found the man standing in the doorway.

Her breath caught again as his eyes sparked. Ria froze. *Mother Goddess, could it be?*

The man had a surprised look on his face that must surely match her own.

Mrs. Tiddle stepped back to admire her work. Her head went from Ria to the man and back again. "Where are my manners? Ty, dear, this is Ria and Dani. They're visiting from a planet called Earth, shopping for the ball."

"The wings were kind of a give away." He nodded and Ria's psi buzzed. "You both look stunning."

"Thanks," Dani said, spinning in front of the mirror, admiring her wings. "This will look perfect next to Ian's tux."

"And we're back to Ian." Ria shook her head, trying to clear the fog that had descended.

Dani gave her a nudge with her psi.

Ria did her own pirouette in front of the mirror. She felt supremely self-conscious knowing that Ty watched her. *Ty.* Could he be the one?

Every ounce of her body thrilled. Stuck in free fall, she could barely breathe.

She watched him in the mirror as he used a metal bar to pry off the rest of the doorframe. His short-sleeved T-shirt showed muscled arms and hinted at a rippled abdomen.

She pictured herself trailing her fingers down his abs and wasn't quite able to stifle a low moan.

Dani grabbed her arm and pulled her to the side. "You're staring...and you're totally flushed." She laughed then. "Got the hots for someone?"

"Shhh. He'll hear you."

"Funny how sound travels in a small, round room." His voice resonated deep inside her.

She smiled at him, totally tongue-tied, which was so not like her.

He reached around the corner and brought in a new plank, affixing it to the frame.

Ria stepped inside her dressing stall and pulled the curtain shut. Her heart pounded in her chest.

Dani stuck her head inside. "You okay?"

Ria let out a laugh. "Yeah, just going to get dressed. Meet me out front?"

Dani gave her a knowing grin. "Sure. I'll leave you alone with Mr. Hottie."

Ria pushed her out and closed the drape again. Funny. The thought had struck her that he could be her psi-mate. What should she say? What should she do? She shrugged out of her dress, being careful not to crush the wings. It was truly beautiful. *I'll get another in green.* She looked good in green. Pulling on her pants, she thought of the man outside. Ty. What if he was vowed to someone? A near panic ripped through her. She shoved her boots on and grabbed her shirt. She didn't know what she was going to say, but she had to say something before he left.

* * * *

Ty watched the petite redhead dart back into the dressing room. He pressed his palms on the plank, setting the adhesive. He turned and leaned his back against the wood, running a hand through his hair. There was no denying the way she made him feel. The way she made his psi feel. He turned and ran his hands along the frame, checking for any loose spots. Even his attraction to Olivia paled in comparison to this. He hadn't made any effort to see her during the last two weeks. Red, here, was nice. More than nice, she made his psi burn with desire. He went to the stall with the broken bench and got to work. A few minutes later, he sensed her presence. She definitely gave him a buzz. He drove the last nail into place. "You should get that dress in emerald green, too. You'd look good in that color." He stood and turned to face her.

She actually blushed. "I was thinking the same thing." Her voice broke, and she cleared her throat a few times.

Ty leaned a shoulder against the wall and crossed his arms. He enjoyed watching her squirm.

"So, I take it you're from here?" she finally asked.

"Born and raised."

She nodded and glanced around the empty dressing room. "Right, well, I guess it was nice meeting you." She turned to go but stopped at the sound of his voice and the pull from his psi.

"We never completed the introductions." He held out his hand. The thought of touching her was extremely appealing. "Ty Sordina."

She stared at his hand. Not moving an inch.

Come on, Red. You know you want to.

She blew out a little laugh. "Ria Montori." She placed her hand in his.

He nearly jumped at the bolt of pleasure that coursed through him. Their eyes met, and the thrill increased. If he didn't let go, he was going to have to take her here and now. From the look of her, she might just beat him to it. He did let go and tilted his head. "I think we need to have dinner. Are you free tonight?"

Her smile spoke to his heart, which really wasn't what he'd intended. *It's only chemistry.* He could tell himself that all he wanted, but the urge to pull her into his arms suggested otherwise.

Chapter 3

A little over an hour later Ria, Dani, and Laric sat at an outdoor table of a very posh restaurant. Ria was having a hard time controlling the butterflies in her stomach. She'd agreed to meet Ty back here at the market at seven-thirty, and she couldn't wait. The energy he'd infused in her was making it difficult to sit still. She tried to focus on the present. The cafe had a lovely outdoor terrace overlooking the bustling market. The sun warmed her skin, and just enough of a breeze blew in from the nearby ocean to keep the temperature perfect. Watersedge smelled of an interesting mix of ocean and earth. A few minutes later, Laric's father and stepmother joined them.

Leon Jara had recently returned from a ten-year stint in the Sandarian military. His stiff posture and crisp dress would have pegged him as a serviceman, even if she hadn't served herself. Laric's stepmother, who went by Nini, was the epitome of what humans would call a trophy wife—closer to Laric's age than Leon's and beautiful.

The three stood, and Laric made the introductions.

Leon had a firm grasp as expected. "You're a surprise. I just assumed there would be a height requirement for EPs."

Ria bit back the irritation that always came with comments like that. "Four years in the Sandarian Academy. Graduated second in class. I can hold my own, sir."

Nini extended a hand. "Don't mind him, honey. He doesn't filter much of what comes out of his mouth."

"No problem." Ria shook the offered hand and stifled a grimace. The only thing worse than a knuckle-busting handshake was one like

Nini's wet noodle. They all took their seats and a waiter swooped in to take drink orders.

"So," Leon said. "Laric tells me the entire Cavacent clan has moved from Sandaria to Earth."

"Yes, we've been there since the emperor's fall," Ria said.

"Ha." Leon leaned back in his chair. "That old Rucon sure pulled a turn there. No one's going to get the carnium away from the Cavacents now. Still, leaving your home planet like that. I hope it's worth it."

Ria wasn't sure how to read Leon. "Politics on Sandaria weren't favorable to the Cavacents, or many others, for that matter."

"That's because he wouldn't play the game." Leon leaned forward and tapped the table in front of Ria. "Man's got to play the game if he wants to win."

Ria figured they hadn't exactly lost but kept her mouth shut on that count. "When the emperor was dethroned, it presented a good opportunity for the Cavacents to establish a base away from all the old politics." The fact that the new president on Sandaria wanted Rucon dead didn't help either. Sandaria had gone from being the center of an empire to just another planet. Granted one that had housed the Portal Masters for hundreds of years, but still just a planet.

Leon leaned even closer and looked Ria, then Dani, in the eye. His voice dropped to a conspiratorial tone. "Rumors have it Rucon somehow took a group of fracking Portal Masters with him. That true?"

Ria wasn't picking up any animosity from the man, but she didn't like his line of questioning. "I'm afraid you'd have to ask Rucon about that."

"Ha." Leon took another large drink and set the glass down. "I might just do that."

"All right Father, we agreed, remember?" Laric asked. "Be nice, and no politics."

It occurred to Ria that Leon wasn't entirely happy about the fall of the empire.

Leon glanced over Ria's shoulder, and his jovial mood snapped into military precision. "If you'll excuse me a moment." He stood and quickly walked to the edge of the patio and down a flight of stairs to the market below.

A young teen stood talking to one of the booth vendors.

Leon grabbed his arm and swung him around.

"Oh, dear," Nini said. "I'm sorry girls. He just can't seem to stop working."

"What's wrong?" Ria asked.

"Must be a Curzan," Laric said.

Below, the boy looked terrified. Leon held him tight as he spoke. A short while later, three security officers arrived. They cuffed the teen and led him away.

Leon returned to the table looking quite pleased.

"Trouble?" Ria asked, curious what just happened.

"Just an out-of-line Curzan. They're getting out of control. It's time we put them back in their place."

Nini reached out and patted his hand.

He looked really tense for such a minor altercation. The rest of lunch was uneventful. Leon said his goodbyes, wishing them luck with their shopping. Nini left for home, telling them to come and go as they pleased.

Ria leaned back in her chair, comfortably full. "That was excellent. Thank you."

"That stew was amazing," Dani agreed.

Laric finished off the wine bottle between their glasses. "I'm glad you liked it. This is one of our favorite restaurants."

"Tell me about the Curzans," Ria said. "Your father seemed really upset."

"Yeah, that boy didn't appear to be doing anything wrong," Dani said.

Laric let out a breath. "Curzans have no legal status on Mitah. They are property, and unless they're running an errand for their masters, they shouldn't be going around on their own."

"Wow. Why are they slaves?"

"The Salvator family was awarded the planetary rulership of Mitah because the native Curzans were about to destroy it. You know how it works."

"Wait," Dani said. "Is that what Rucon is on Earth? A planetary ruler?"

"No." Ria shook her head. "Rucon has a protectorship, not a rulership. That could change if Earth starts destroying itself."

"Huh. Learn something new every day," Dani said.

"Your father really doesn't like Curzans, does he?" Ria asked.

Laric placed his elbows on the table. "No, he doesn't. You'll have to forgive him." Laric traced his finger on the table. "I had a younger sister. He loved her, doted on her. She died because she was exposed to a Curzan virus. A virus brought to her school by a family who pretended to be Mitan. So, yes. He hates them with a passion."

"Gods, I'm sorry Laric," Ria said.

"It was a long time ago, but he'll never forget or forgive. He and my mother couldn't get past it. They divorced shortly after. When he met Nini, and she gave him twins, he seemed to get better, but the anger is never far from the surface."

"Are the twins at home?" Ria asked.

"No. Boarding school. You'll meet them when you return for the ball."

"What about that boy?" Dani asked. "He's just a kid. What's going to happen to him?"

Laric didn't answer. Just shrugged and shook his head.

* * * *

Later that night, Ria stood in front of the mirror in Jara's guest room.

Dani was kicked back on the bed, flipping through local magazines on her com. "You look fantastic."

"Thanks." She had to agree. The ankle-length black pants, strappy sandals, and a cream-colored silk shirt all combined to highlight her red hair. "Sorry for abandoning you like this. Are you sure you don't mind?"

"Of course not. Go and have fun. You deserve it. I've got a nice long call planned with Ian."

Ria rolled her eyes. "Well I certainly don't need to be around for that."

An hour later, she stood in the open-air market and marveled at the lights. The energy and excitement here was palpable, not to mention the butterflies cavorting in her stomach. There was no sign of Ty yet, so she wandered about the market. Crews of men and women decorated for the ball. They laughed and joked as they worked. The ball was enormous, and it took time to put it all together. Beautiful luminescent spheres of blue, green, and purple floated fifteen feet in the air, casting a dreamy glow over the stalls and people milling about.

A vendor caught her eye and waved a handful of flowing, glowing material in her direction. "Pretty lady, I have scarves for you." He rifled through the scarves. "A red one here to match your hair. Come, pretty lady. I make a deal for you. Fifteen credits. Only for you."

"It's worth two, if that." Ty's voice sent a warm breath down her neck, igniting her insides.

She spun around and found him smiling at her. He wasn't much taller than her, and she couldn't help but imagine how their bodies would fit together. It had been too long since she'd been with a man. And she wanted this one.

"Is that all? Surely it's worth more than two credits." She walked over to the vendor and took the scarf he offered. She'd been told how the silk came alive in the dark and the sheer fabric was stunning. "My friend here says it's not worth more than two credits."

"Bah. I'd wager your friend there doesn't have four mouths to feed at home."

Ty laughed beside her. He whispered in her ear. "He's got a point. Offer him five and no more. Wait." He reached out and pulled a shimmering green scarf from the pile. "The color of your eyes."

Ria pulled out her com. "I'll pay you ten."

Both men made exasperated noises, which made her laugh.

"It's robbery, but for you, pretty lady, okay." He held his com out and Ria sent over the credits.

She draped the scarf over her shoulders and turned to Ty. "What do you think?"

A beat of silence before he replied, "Ravishing."

He held out his arm, and she looped her hand around it. He wore a long-sleeved button-up shirt, which hid the muscles that had been on such delicious display earlier in the day. She tightened her grip on his bicep and felt the impressive bulge underneath the fabric. He led her away from the center of the market and down a narrower cobblestone alley. Like the market, it was closed to vehicles. Light from shop fronts and cafes reflected off the smooth stones. Music and laughter surrounded them, and the colored orbs that hovered overhead gave the night a festive feel.

Ty flexed his arm to get her attention. "Where are you from again?"

She nearly said Sandaria, but caught herself. She wasn't from there anymore. "Earth."

"Haven't heard of it."

"There's really no reason why you would. It's a little blue planet not much larger than this one."

He motioned to the side and held the door open to a small restaurant. She stepped through and inhaled deeply. It smelled amazing and reminded her of the villa's kitchen when Gina was cooking. Candlelit tables dotted the small cozy space.

A plump woman wiped her hands on her apron and hurried over. "Ty! So good of you to come. I saved the table by the window for you and your friend." The woman got them situated. Before leaving them, she leaned over and said loud enough to be overheard, "She's a lovely one." She winked at Ria and returned to the kitchen.

The evening flew by. Ty was funny and kept her laughing. They flirted and became increasingly intimate as the night wore on. Finally, with the bill paid, they stood to leave. He placed his hand at the small of her back, sending her stomach into a flutter, and led her outside. They stopped under the light of the moons and faced each other. He took her hand in his and traced circles in her palm. Her breath quickened as the touch sent swirls of pleasure up her arm and resonated with her psi.

"I like you, Red." His voice was low and husky.

"I like you, too." Liked the way he called her Red.

"Stay with me tonight." He paused before adding. "Just so we're clear, I can't commit to anything right now, but I'd love for you to stay with me tonight."

Ria smiled. She couldn't have asked for a more perfect arrangement. She was hot, wet, and ready for this man. All she wanted was to rip his clothes off and press her body against his. "Right now it's not commitment I'm looking for."

His smile was melt-worthy. He lifted the corner of her scarf and brushed it against her cheek. "It really does match your eyes." Grasping her hand in his, he then led the way down the cobblestoned alley. In the few short blocks to his apartment, they didn't speak a word, but the glances they shared spoke volumes. He led her up a flight of wooden stairs and wrapped his arms around her waist. "Last chance to change your mind. Once you step through that door, there's no going back." He wore a sexy, evil grin.

She was wound so tight in anticipation, leaving wasn't an option. She slipped her arms around his neck and lost herself in those lips of his.

Ty opened the door to his flat with his psi, and they tumbled inside. His tongue ignited her passion to a frenzy. Shoes, shirts, and pants scattered as they raced to undress. He beat her by a fraction of a second and stood with hands on hips, waiting for her.

Hopping on one foot, she yanked her pants off and caught her breath as she took him in. She stood upright and twirled her finger, motioning for him to turn around.

He obliged with a crooked grin.

Magnificent. He had a wicked curve at the small of his back and a tight ass. Muscled thighs framed his erection, which pulsed with his desire for her.

"Your turn."

She turned slowly. She and the other EPs trained everyday, and she was proud of her figure.

He closed the distance between them and placed his hands on her hips, thumbs brushing over her abdomen. "You're amazing."

She wrapped her arms around his neck and resumed their kiss. Their bodies fit together perfectly, just as she'd imagined. With each kiss, her thoughts subsided and pleasure reigned. Heart pounding, he led her into his bedroom. He flipped the covers back with his psi and they fell into the soft mattress. Every inch of him was hard as she wrapped her hand around his erection.

He moaned and bit down on her shoulder as she pumped up and down. His hands roamed her body, finally descending to her thighs.

She opened her legs wider, desperate for his touch.

His fingers circled around her mound.

Begging with her body, she lifted her hips.

"Is this what you want?" He flicked her clit.

She growled. "I need you in me."

His fingers circled wider, spreading her wetness.

Each touch sent insane pulses of pleasure coursing through her, and a cry escaped her lips as he plunged his fingers deep inside. His mouth claimed hers, and his tongue matched the rhythm of his fingers.

It was fucking erotic and intense. She bucked her hips and pumped him faster. The thickness of his cock registered in her pleasure-fogged brain, and she was done waiting. She needed him now.

In one fluid motion, she pushed him backward, straddled his body, and sank onto him. He matched her intake of breath as their psi pulsed with pleasure that exploded over and through them.

Sparks of light flashed in his gray eyes as she slid on and off him. He grabbed her hips and slammed her onto him with more force. They moved faster, in and out. Each plunge brought her closer to the release she desperately needed.

She placed her hands on either side of his shoulders. Covered in a fine sheen of perspiration, her breasts swung with their increasing rhythm. The tightening started deep within. "Yes." She closed her eyes and arched her back as he pounded into her. And pushed her over the razor's edge.

She clenched the sheets and called out as the orgasm exploded. Once, twice, three more plunges, and Ty moaned out his own release. The pleasure didn't stop. It rolled on and on and echoed around their psi. She took a deep breath and opened her eyes.

He stared back at her. Neither of them moved or said a word. There were no words. Ria didn't know what that was, but it wasn't what she expected. It was pure ecstasy, and it was crazy.

Without leaving her body, Ty rolled her over and propped himself up on his elbows as she wrapped her legs around his waist. He tightened his abs and plunged deeper inside her, already hardening again. Their tryst had taken on a serious note, the pleasure still rippling through their psi.

He shifted his weight to one side and brushed a strand of hair from her face. The touch was gentle, and his look questioning. Slowly, he moved in and out of her. She could get lost in those gray depths. A string of pleasure stirred between her legs, forcing a moan from her lips.

He shifted back on top of her and increased his tempo.

Mother Goddess, what was he doing to her?

Chapter 4

Ty woke the next morning to the sound of clothes rustling. He propped himself up and watched Ria pull on her pants.

"Sorry," she said, "I was trying not to wake you."

"It's all right." He watched in silence as she left the room and returned a moment later with a handful of clothes.

She stepped into the wisp of a thong. "I think next time, I'll try to keep my clothes in the bedroom." She froze as soon as the words were out and cast a flustered look at him. "I mean, if there is a next time. Not that I'm assuming there will be."

"I think I'd like a next time." He sat up and leaned against the headboard.

She continued dressing. She really was perfect. A small, tight package with handful-sized breasts. They'd gone till the small hours of the morning before falling asleep, exhausted and well sated.

She sat on the side of the bed to pull on her sandals.

He resisted the urge to reach out to her. Something had shifted last night. He was pretty sure she felt it, too. Hooking up for mutual benefit was one thing. What they did last night? That was different. Was it possible they could have more? The thought scared the shit out of him, and he swung his legs off the bed and pulled his jeans on.

"Can I get you some caff before you go?" Part of him wanted her to stay, but only a part. His life didn't lend itself to a long-term relationship. Or maybe it could. Hell, he didn't know. His focus had always been on their cause. On freedom. How would she feel if she knew the truth? No. He couldn't take that chance.

"Thanks, but I need to get back. More shopping to do today before we leave."

They stood looking at each other, suddenly awkward.

Ty's com signaled from the other room. He pinged it with his psi to see who it was. *Olivia.* "I need to, um—"

"Go ahead. Take it. I'll see myself out." She pulled her hair into a tie and hurried out the door.

"Shit." Ty picked up the com and connected. "Hey, Olivia. What's up?" He watched the door close and felt a pull on his psi. *Shit.*

Her voice came through loud and clear, but she may as well have spoken a foreign language. He hadn't heard a word she said. "Sorry. What did you say?"

"Wake up, will you? I said I'll be in town for a few hours today. You want to have lunch?"

No, he didn't. "Yeah, sure. How about the cafe on Rue Street?"

"Perfect." She sounded way too happy. "See you around one?"

"Yeah. See you then." He disconnected and stared at the door. He wanted to go after Ria. "Frack." He spun around and put a caff module in the maker. He was kidding himself if he thought they had a chance. She'd find out he was Curzan, and it would be over. Hell, she might even turn him in. No. She wasn't an option.

* * * *

Ty's mood hadn't improved by the time lunch rolled around. It didn't help that Olivia was uncharacteristically chipper. They sat at an outdoor table a few blocks from the square. Ty found himself watching all the people passing by. Looking, waiting for a redhead.

"Are you okay?" Olivia said around a mouth full of salad.

He was starting to wonder that himself. "I didn't sleep much last night." That much was true.

"Hum. So I take it you don't want to, you know…" Her almond shaped eyes took on a smoky look.

He nearly coughed up his bread. The thought of sleeping with her now was freakishly repulsive. Which didn't make sense. They had a long history of hooking up. What was wrong with him? "Sorry. Not today."

She finished her bite. "Is that why you didn't get much sleep last night?"

His long pause was answer enough.

She pursed her lips. "It's not like I have any exclusive hold on you. Anyone I know?" She stabbed her food with more force than necessary.

"No. Just a tourist visiting from a planet called Earth."

Olivia stopped chewing and swallowed hard. "Did you say Earth?"

"Yeah, why?"

"That can't be right. You must have misheard."

"I'm pretty sure she said Earth." Ty didn't like the look on Olivia's face. "What's wrong with Earth? And how do you know about it, anyway?"

"Because, unlike some people, I pay attention to what's going on in the galaxy, not just our world." As the daughter of the leader of the Starfall Underground, she was well connected. Their underground was the largest and most comprehensive on the planet.

Ty's anger flared, but she was right. He didn't pay too much attention to things going on beyond Mitah. He knew the big stuff. The emperor was dethroned, and there was a new Galactic Trade Organization in its place. So what? It hadn't made any difference here.

"She can't be from Earth, because it's a dark planet. That, and they don't have psi."

Dark planets had yet to explore the stars and didn't know about the network of planets that comprised the former empire. As for not having psi… "Oh, she had psi all right." His heart pounded at the memory of the pleasure she gave him. "And you know about Earth how?"

"It's only one of the major suppliers of carnium. Gods, Ty. You really need to pay more attention."

Ty knew interstellar ships used carnium, but that had nothing to do with him.

Olivia pulled up her com and started searching. "Here it is. Earth is the third largest source for carnium." She mumbled a few things, scanning the data stream. "Earthlings have no psi. I told you."

It didn't make sense. "I'm telling you, she had psi."

Olivia continued reading. "This is interesting. One of the major clans on Sandaria moved to Earth after the fall of the Emperor. Lord Rucon Cavacent. Was she a Cavacent?"

"I don't remember her last name, but it wasn't Cavacent."

"Maybe she's married."

"She's not married." It came out harsher than he'd intended.

She gave him a quizzical look. "Well, she's not human either. Here." She projected the source she was reading. "Any of these look familiar?"

It started with Lord Rucon and his wife Mara. Their son, Ian. An uncle…" Ty scrolled down to a list of Earth Protectors. His heart beat double time when he saw her face. "It's her."

Olivia zoomed in and pulled up the bio. "Frack, Ty. She's ex-military."

Ty felt sucker punched. It was a Sandarian military officer that had killed his parents. His anger nearly blinded him. He put a handful of credits on the table and left without a word. Rage coursed through his veins as he walked. Ria was not only a Sandarian, but ex-military. It explained her physique. *But it doesn't explain what she did to me.* It made him insane to think he'd just slept with his worst enemy, and it had been the best sex of his life. The thought that it might have been more than sex had his stomach turning.

* * * *

Ty finished the repairs on the tall wooden stool and used his psi to flip it upright. Wiping his hands on his gray T-shirt, he sent a narrow stream of the energy into the old man next to him. He hadn't known it was possible until a few months back. He'd shown up to do some repairs and found Jafferies hunched over and looking like hell. It was instinct. He fed psi into the man while he made him tea and talked non-stop so he wouldn't notice.

You wouldn't approve would you, old man?

Jafferies was stubborn, proud, and dying.

"That will hold her." Ty slid the stool aside with his foot. He'd take it out front as soon as he'd pumped a little more psi into the man's frail body. "Anything else while I'm here?"

Jafferies's head trembled a little less than it had earlier. "Nothing today," he said in a raspy voice. "But don't worry. I'm sure something else will break before too long." He ticked off items on his inventory sheet. "You'll be wanting store credit as usual?"

"Yeah. I told Trin she could have it. I still eat over there half the time, anyway."

Jafferies chuckled. "I would, too, if I was you. Your mom can cook."

A brief look passed between the two men.

Trin and Merek Sordina took him in when he was just ten. He'd been coming here ever since. He used to do odd jobs around the shop after school for extra credits.

"Sorry, boy." Jafferies gave him a sad look. "You know what I mean."

"It's all right. She's like a mother to me." Ty pushed his black bangs off his face.

Jafferies had owned the small neighborhood supplies store since before Ty was born. The disease that racked the storeowner's body was in the end stages, and he didn't have long to live. Ever practical, he already had a buyer lined up for when he passed. Ty's jaw clenched when he thought of the Sandarian medicine that could have cured him. As part of the Sandarian Empire, Mitah had full access to its medicines and technology.

The door out front chimed, and a moment later a male voice rang out, "Jafferies Orlander. By order of Chancellor Mortog, you will submit for DNA testing at once."

Ty grabbed Jafferies's arm. "Come on, we have to get out of here."

With surprising strength, Jafferies pulled back. "No, son." The old man put down his inventory sheet. "You have to get out. I've been expecting this. They're finding us, you know, one by one." He placed his hand over Ty's. "You need to figure out how they're doing it."

Over the last six months, two families, consisting of four Curzans and one Mitan, had been executed. That event had shattered over ten years of relative quiet and safety.

"No." Ty ran a hand through his hair. "I'm not letting you do this."

Jafferies's voice was steady and proud. "My time is up, son. You're young, and our people need you. We're counting on you to lead the long fight, the important fight, the one that sees Curzans on equal ground as Mitans." Jafferies squared his shoulders and stood tall. He gave Ty a quizzical look. "Huh. You been doing something to me? Haven't felt this good in some time."

Ty shrugged.

"Well that's good, then." Jafferies straightened his shirt. "I could use a little help with what I'm about to do."

"Jafferies—"

"No." He held up a hand. "You tell Trin and Merek I went out with my head held high. As a Curzan."

Ty shook with anger. The man was in constant pain and had a right to die as he chose.

As Jafferies turned toward the front of the store, Merek burst into the back room from the alley. He covered the space between them and grabbed ahold of Ty's arm.

Jafferies smiled and saluted the two men before pushing through the swinging door.

"What's he doing?" Merek hissed. "Do you know who's out there?"

"He said—" Ty froze at the sight on the other side. Standing near the cash machine was a ghost from his past. It wore the uniform of the chancellor's private security team. Fifteen years ago, the uniform had been that of the Sandarian military, but the man was the same.

For an instant, Ty was a child again, sitting in a small schoolroom with the other kids. The last moments of his parents' lives before the man who stood out front had killed them. His childhood ended that day as he watched, helpless. For a moment, Ty locked eyes with the devil himself.

The door swung shut, leaving only the small window view.

"Come on, we have to leave." Merek pulled at his arm.

"Wait." Ty shrugged free and ran to the window.

Merek mumbled something under his breath, but came to stand behind Ty, peering through the old window over his shoulder.

On the shop floor, Jafferies raised his hands, gathered the remains of his psi, and pushed outward.

The chancellor's deputy flew backward and slammed into the shelves. It was an awkward impact. His head smacked against boxes of *shrack* poison, and his feet dangled a few feet off the ground. As though in response, two of the furry shracks scurried out from underneath the shelves and darted across the floor.

Ty knew how this would end, but he couldn't pull away.

The look of shock on the deputy's face quickly turned to rage.

Jafferies staggered with the strain of keeping the man pinned. "I'm not afraid of you, monster," his voice rang out. "You're taking the life of an already dying and forever proud Curzan." Jafferies's body gave a final great heave, and his hands dropped to his sides.

The official slid to the floor, landing on his feet.

With the last of his strength, Jafferies proclaimed, "In the light of our Mother Goddess, I forgive you for what you are about to do."

Ty caught his breath, and Merek grabbed his arms, preventing him from moving. Neither man could tear away from the scene playing out in front of them.

The deputy pushed himself off the teetering rack. Sneering, he withdrew a weapon holstered on his outer thigh. "Save it for someone who cares." Stepping forward, he activated a short laser blade and sliced off Jafferies's head with a smooth flick of his wrist. Blood spurted out, and the man stepped aside to avoid the mess as the elderly man crumpled to the floor.

Merek yanked Ty backward, covering his mouth with a massive palm.

Ty tried to free himself and go after the killer, but Merek had a good forty-five pounds and at least a foot on him. Merek heaved him out the back door and into a waiting cruiser.

Ty flailed and roared as the two crashed to the floor. The cruiser sped off on auto. Merek pinned him down, a grimace on his reddened face.

Ty bellowed out his rage until Merek finally let him go. He flipped over and crouched, ready to attack his adoptive father. "He didn't have to die." His throat hurt from screaming.

Merek climbed to a seat, breathing heavy. "He was already dying. He died his way, with pride." He paused a beat, raising an eyebrow. "You gonna calm down, boy? Or you gonna take a swing at me?"

Ty slammed his fists to the floor on either side of him before maneuvering into a seat that faced Merek. He leaned forward, elbows on knees. A quick look around told him they were headed to one of the underground's safe spots. He took a few breaths, trying to quell his anger. He'd searched for years for that killer to no avail. *I don't know where you've been, but I will find you.* He looked to Merek. "How did you know he was there?"

"Our boys flagged his uniform when he came into town. They were keeping an eye on him and called me as soon as he showed up at the store." Merek leaned in and swatted Ty's knee. "You okay now?"

Ty's hands shook from the adrenalin rush. "Yeah."

Merek was a giant of a man with a kind face. Ty wasn't sure how things would have ended today if he hadn't shown up.

"Thanks, Merek."

"You're welcome, but you've really got to watch that temper of yours," Merek said. "We need you. Getting yourself killed isn't going to help our cause any."

"I know." Ty gritted his teeth. His life had gone down a twisted path. First the Sandarian military *crag*, Ria, and now this. None of it mattered anymore. He knew what he had to do.

Chapter 5

Balastar Alder finished filing his customs forms and flicked on the view screen. He leaned back in his captain's chair and enjoyed the scene. They orbited Florin 5. A fascinating planet whose designers had built their cities with the view from space in mind. Interconnected geometric patterns glittered below, but he'd been here before and knew the facade to be largely illusion. On the surface, the majority of inhabitants lived in poverty, and many of the massive structures stood abandoned or taken over by squatters. Still, those who had credits tended to have a lot. It was an active trade planet with a thriving entertainment industry.

A message flashed on his com indicating the contents of the ship's holds had been transferred to the planet-side spaceport. The cargo would work its way through customs, then they'd start loading the new shipments. The whole process would take a day, maybe two, tops. Building his own transport business would take time, but with Rucon Cavacent's support, he wasn't worried. Besides, time was something he had plenty of. A broken heart was a damn good motivator to get out and change your life.

He scratched the day's old stubble on his chin. He'd fallen hard and fast for Dani Standich, the beautiful human who somehow possessed psi. After she and Ian bonded back on Sandaria, he bowed out. Balastar knew she cared a great deal for him, that much was clear, but a bond was a bond.

He and the Cavacent clan had barely escaped that planet with their lives. Although Earth was his home now, he spent little time there. He busied himself learning his new profession inside and out. A far cry from his old life as the youngest Sandarian Council member, he now captained his own transport ship, ferrying goods from one planet to another. His life was new and exhilarating, seeing different worlds and all the experiences that went along with the job. Not to mention a few women he'd come to know in different ports. He'd yet to encounter any space pirates, but the ship was heavily armed. That was enough of a deterrent for most.

This run was a little different. He had company. Rucon's brother, Mordo, and the leader of the now rogue Portal Masters, Durgan. EP Marco Dar had also come along to protect the Portal Master. Balastar shook his head. His gut told him that Marco could be deadly if needed, but the man's natural state was one of comic affability. Every afternoon, when Mordo and Durgan returned from their expeditions hunting for the newly discovered form of psi, Marco would go back out. How many women the EP had slept with in the past two months was anybody's guess. He returned to the ship late, got up early, and did it again the next day, his smile never fading.

Balastar's com alerted him to the approaching shuttle. Mordo and Durgan could only canvas the locals for an hour at a time before needing rest. The process drained their psi quickly.

"You're back early." Balastar turned to greet them as they entered the bridge. "Get tired of planet-side food?" He bolted to his feet when he saw the look on their faces.

Mordo and Durgan were both shaken. Having given up the standard Portal Master robes, Durgan now dressed in regular clothes, slacks and button-up shirts. Mordo sported his usual black cloak, his skin unusually pale in contrast.

Marco followed them onto the bridge with a serious expression. "We had a little altercation."

Durgan nodded. "It appears Gordat Prayda has placed a bounty on my head."

The newly elected president of Sandaria was an old enemy of the Cavacent clan, but what he'd want with a Portal Master, Balastar couldn't guess. "What happened?"

"I persuaded the bounty hunter to look elsewhere," Marco said with a grin.

Balastar activated his com and did a quick search. The hit was almost immediate. He sent the results to the vid for the others to see. Durgan Serred and the other eight Portal Masters that had defected with him were wanted men.

Balastar shook his head. "He wants the Portal Masters dead?"

"Alive," Marco said. "That much was clear. If he'd wanted them dead, Durgan here would be."

"I don't understand," Balastar said to Durgan. "Why would Prayda want you returned to Sandaria?"

"I doubt Prayda is behind the hit." Durgan frowned. "I'm quite sure the Portal Masters are pulling the strings."

"They want you back?" Balastar asked.

Mordo and Durgan shared a glance. "It would appear so. Although we are not clear as to why they would go to such lengths. We are less than a quarter of the guild."

"A quarter," Balastar said. "I always assumed there were more of you."

"Apprentices yes, but not full masters. Few make it past the fourth year."

"Looks like your hunting days are over, my friends." Balastar killed the feed to the vid.

"Over, perhaps," Durgan said. "But not in vain."

"You found someone?" Balastar asked.

"Not someone," Mordo said.

"Something," Durgan finished, holding out a small black box.

Balastar took the device. It was identical to the one Armond used to create portals. In theory, there were people in existence that possessed an alternate form of psi. With the help of the rogue Portal Masters, they could use the device to create interstellar portals. It was these people who Mordo and Durgan were searching for. As for the devices, now plural, they had no idea where they came from. As far as they knew, being able to create interstellar portals without the guild had never happened before. Interesting times, to be sure. "Where did you get it?" He handed the device back to Durgan.

"Sitting in a vendor's cart at an open air market. We'd just purchased it for next to nothing when the bounty hunter appeared."

"How did he find you?"

"*She* found him by pure luck," Marco said. "Kept tossing around Gordat Prayda's name like it meant something, so I mentioned Supreme Commander Torril Anantha, and we came to an understanding."

Balastar cocked his head. "Have you met Commander Anantha?"

Marco flashed his boyish grin. "Not exactly, but I figure Rucon's relationship with him is close enough."

"Well played. I'll report to Rucon." He turned to Mordo and Durgan. "I'd prefer you not leave the ship again until we get back to Earth. We can depart as soon as my current contracts are loaded."

"They ain't going anywhere on my watch." Marco crossed his arms.

Mordo sighed. "Agreed. Let Rucon know of our findings. We're going to contact Armond and arrange a meeting as soon as we arrive."

"All right." Marco rubbed his hands together. "If no one needs me, I'm going back planet-side. I know a certain bounty hunter who needs consoling."

* * * *

Nearly a week after Jafferies's death, Ty sat in Merek and Trin's small but immaculate kitchen. It was fifteen years to the day since his parents were killed.

He toyed with the crust of his sandwich as sun streamed through the lace curtains behind the sink. The anniversary always brought sadness to the Sordina household. Ty hadn't wanted to come, but staying away would have broken Trin's heart.

"How's Father Arlo today?" Trin asked.

"He's fine," Ty said. "The underground took in that family he mentioned last night. I told him we'd let the boy work in the shop if he wanted. I assume that's all right?"

"Sure." Merek took a bite of his sandwich.

A slight ocean breeze ruffled the leaves on the trees outside the window.

Fifteen years. He'd lived with his adoptive parents for twelve of those, but moved out three years ago when Bella had arrived. Not far, just a private space to call his own. The Sordina house was small, and at fifteen, Bella needed them now more than he did.

One of Father Arlo's oldest friends had owned Bella and her real parents. A priest as well, he'd educated the family, and Bella, especially, took to books, languages, and math. When the priest had fallen ill and died, the church was assigned a new pastor. One with strong political aspirations and far less generous views of Curzans. Bella was to be sold as soon as she turned twelve, which at the time, was only weeks away.

When Arlo had gotten word, the Watersedge underground went into action. They had traveled four hundred miles to the west and smuggled her out. Like Ty before her, she had assumed the position of the child of Merek and Trin. Arlo and Merek had spent the last twenty-five years growing their community on the edge of town. More Curzans were finding mates among the Mitan population. The lines were blurring. Despite the new edict of the Galactic Trade Organization to treat all psi-abled and non psi-abled as equals, the Mitah government lived in the past, and the GTO had more important battles to fight.

Ty tore the crust off his sandwich and set it aside.

Trin repositioned her plate. "You should let me cut your hair while you're here. It's long overdue, you know."

She was right. "Maybe tomorrow."

Trin pushed her untouched plate away. "I'm sorry, Ty. I shouldn't have insisted you come today. I just hate the thought of you being alone."

"It's all right," Ty said. "To be honest, I can't stop thinking about Jafferies."

"Gods, I know. That was an evil thing to do." Trin placed her hand on Merek's, who sat next to her. "Maybe we should leave Mitah. Find another planet to call home. I have a cousin on Tondor. We could all go there. I'm sure she'd help us."

"We've been over this," Merek said. "It would cost every credit we have. No. This is our home. The emperor is gone. It's a new day."

Trin closed her eyes, a pained expression on her face. "Not on Mitah, it isn't. Not with Chancellor Mortog's henchmen killing Curzans simply because they choose to educate themselves. What if they find us, or little Bella? She's only fifteen. Dear Goddess, I couldn't live with that."

Merek squeezed her hand. "Don't think like that. You've got to stay positive and look to the future. We have the books and the journals. Father Arlo is sure he and Ty and Bella are making progress."

Trin pulled her hand back and twisted her napkin. "You three have been at it for two years. What if there's nothing to find?"

"We are making progress," Ty said. "Once we formulate the key, it's going to crack wide open. Every word will be ours to read." He wanted to add that it wouldn't make any difference. Chancellor Mortog would never let the information get out, but Merek believed if they could prove the original Curzans had psi, the planetary rulership would be defunct. Planets with psi-abled citizens could not be governed by non-natives. And Mitah had psi-abled citizens. In theory, if they could prove they'd been here all along and weren't the product of inbreeding, they could go to the GTO and revoke the rulership. In theory. Repeated attempts to reach out had failed and Mortog was determined to keep the status quo.

Ty stood and hugged the back of her shoulders. He picked up the plates and carried them over to the sink where Merek joined him.

Trin remained sitting, tracing the design on her cold cup of tea.

They put the food in the fridge for later.

"I'll call you tomorrow, okay?" Ty said. "Tell Bella I said hi."

Trin simply nodded, her shoulders slumped forward.

Merek followed him downstairs, through the woodworking and furniture shop where Ty also worked, and out into the warm day. They stood on Merek's small deck. The two moons were clearly visible in the sky. The smell of the ocean, mixed with the nearby forest, brought both comfort and painful memories.

The school where his birth parents had taught the local Curzan children lay deep in the forest. Ty had never found out how they were discovered. His gut clenched at the memory.

Leon Jara.

He and fourteen other kids watched as Jara and his men burst in and murdered his parents. When the screams of the younger kids died down, Jara had turned to the class and told them if he ever caught any Curzans trying to *learn something* again, he would personally hunt them down and kill them and their families. And then Jara and his men left, his parents' bodies bleeding out on the old wood floor. Ty hadn't seen any of those kids since, but he'd heard more than a few had gone missing.

Traffic meandered along the road at the bottom of the hill. Over the treetops, the ocean beyond the cliffs sparkled.

Ty scanned the area. In a low voice he said, "I know who he is."

"Who?" Merek asked.

"The man who killed Jafferies. His name is Leon Jara." Ty turned and looked Merek in the eyes. "He's the one who killed my parents."

Merek sucked in a breath. "How—? Why—?"

"Olivia Zar. Her underground's infiltration of the government in Starfall is extensive. She was able to find out who he is. Apparently, Jara doesn't like the new direction the GTO is taking, so he came home to pick up where he left off."

"Oh, Ty. I'm so sorry."

"He's been serving in the Sandarian military." He couldn't think about the military without a certain redhead invading his memories. "Jara's going to the ball, of course." Ty looked away. "I know what he'll be wearing, who he'll be with, and where their reserved table on the lawn is located."

Merek bowed his head and leaned forward, palms on the pristine white rail he'd made himself. "Don't do anything rash. Our underground needs you."

Ty knew the older man didn't want to hear the truth. "It's time to start our war."

"It doesn't have to happen like this. There are the texts…and when Zander Salvator returns from university, Mortog will lose his power. Zander's father was a good man. Is a good man, I suppose."

Anton Salvator, Planetary Ruler of Mitah, had not been seen in years. A degenerative brain disease had turned him into nothing more than a shell. In the years leading up to the official announcement, Chancellor Mortog took control of Mitah. Gradually, and with great patience, he'd instilled a network of corrupt officials across the planet. From what Ty could tell, they were hell-bent on wiping out any and all educated Curzans.

"Zander hasn't been here in two years," Ty said.

"He's coming to the ball."

Ty rocked on the balls of his feet. "So? He's only twenty-two. Still has a final year at university, and we have no idea what he thinks about Curzans. And if he is sympathetic to us?" Ty shrugged. "He may not survive his return. Do you really think Mortog will just step aside?"

Merek straightened up. "Don't do this, Ty. You're only twenty-five. You can't come back from killing a man. Besides, Jara is just following orders."

"Orders from Mortog, who underestimates both our numbers and our intelligence."

Merek looked pale and old. "And what if they capture you?"

"They won't." He sounded far more confident than he felt, but the truth was, he didn't care.

* * * *

Ria found the background hum of space travel to be calming. Maybe because it meant the engines were running and the air circulating. Both good things in space. She and Dani were again aboard one of Rucon's well-appointed transport ships headed back to Mitah. This time they had Ian and Armond with them, as well as Ian's parents, Rucon and Mara. Ian's father was at a table in back talking on his com, his mother on the couch near the others. Ria wished Marco could have made it back in time. He always brought an element of comedy to the group. Unfortunately, he wasn't scheduled to be back on Earth for another week.

Supreme Commander Torril Anantha had kept his word, and there was an additional battleship stationed near Earth in their absence. If Torogs or any other aliens tried to visit Earth, they'd get a surprise welcome.

Oversize chairs and couches gave the deck a comfortable, home-like feel. Landscape paintings of various planets adorned the smooth steel walls. Ria rapidly flipped through visitor information about Mitah on her holo-vid. "So, the capital of Mitah is Starfall because that's where the first Sandarians touched down, and party town is Watersedge because it overlooks the Marul Ocean. Not very imaginative with their naming conventions, were they?"

Dani, who'd also been reading up on the planet, agreed. "Apparently Gondor Salvator, the original planetary ruler, preferred function over form. I still find the whole planetary ruler thing bizarre. Could the Curzans ever get the planet back?"

"Why should they?" Armond said, in a haughty tone. "If Sandarians had not intervened, Curzans wouldn't exist. The only reason the rulership was awarded in the first place is because they were on the verge of destroying themselves along with their world."

"Non-psi beings," Rucon said, joining the group and sitting next to his wife, "only get one chance at destroying themselves."

"Wait a minute." Dani looked perplexed. "If the natives are Curzans, why isn't that the planet name?"

"It was, long ago," Armond said. "Salvator changed it."

"Pfft." Dani smirked. "Must be nice being able to walk around changing the names of planets."

Rucon chuckled at that. "I just spoke with Balastar."

"Any luck finding more people with the new form of psi?" Dani asked.

"In a roundabout way. They found another device."

"Seriously? Where?" Ria tuned to Rucon.

"At an open-air market on Florin 5. They purchased it for half a credit. The thing is useless unless you know what it is."

"And have our psi," Armond said.

Ria was a little jealous. Ian, Dani, Armond, and Mara all had the strange psi that would eventually allow them to make portals with the mystery boxes. "It's hard to wrap my head around the thought of you guys creating portals."

"Indeed," Rucon said. "Question is, how did it get on Florin 5?"

"Did they find any people?" Armond asked.

"No, but they had to cut their search short," Rucon said. "Prayda has placed bounties on all the Portal Masters that escaped with us to Earth. They're heading home as soon as Balastar finishes up."

"How's he doing?" Dani asked.

Rucon smiled. "He's found his calling. Piloting a transport ship around the galaxy agrees with him."

"I'm glad," Dani said.

Ian placed his arm around Dani's shoulder. Dani's long blond hair was a few shades lighter than his. Tall and lean, they were a striking couple.

Ria smirked. Their intimacy was cute in a nauseating kind of way. All you had to do was mention Balastar's name, and Ian instinctively reached out to his psi-mate. Ian had known Dani and Balastar were getting closer before he had bonded with her.

Ria checked the time. They'd be on Mitah in a few hours. They were staying with an old friend of Rucon's, Darl Karton and his wife. Ria was looking forward to the Summer's Ball. Beings came from around the galaxy to celebrate life in a party that lasted three days.

A three-day party—Ria stretched out her legs in front of her—*sounds good to me.* She thought back to her night with Ty and hoped she'd see him again. She nudged Armond's boot with her psi. "How's it going with that thing?"

Armond held the portal-making device. "There have been no further revelations regarding its functionality. Ian is making progress. He should be able to create a portal soon."

Ria was tempted to mimic his formal speech but decided to let it go. "Where are you going to place the portal?"

Rucon answered the question. "We'll activate it between Darl's place and your villa. We can always move it later."

Ria hoped they didn't move it. If she managed to find Ty again...the thought was appealing.

"How about Sandaria?" Ria stood, time to get ready. "Any new developments there?"

"Nothing new." Rucon stood as well. The others in the room followed suit. "Gordat and the Portal Masters are playing at something, but we don't know what. What's more interesting is the situation on Mitah."

"What situation?" Ria and Dani chimed in at once.

"Our host, Darl, thinks there's a storm brewing. Native Curzans are being murdered without apparent cause or retribution. There was a death recently in Watersedge, not far from his estate, so he did a little digging. What he discovered didn't make sense. The man had lived in Watersedge for over thirty years, but not as a Curzan. He was well known as a Mitan."

Ria exchanged a look with Dani. "Laric's father mentioned something about the Curzans being out of control."

Rucon eyed her. "Out of control doesn't give anyone the right to kill."

"Agreed," Ria said.

Dani turned to Ria. "What about the boy Leon had taken away?"

"What boy?" Rucon asked.

"Jara went after someone at lunch when we were here last," Ria said.

"And what happened?"

"Jara had him arrested. He was just a teen." It annoyed Ria that he'd interrupted lunch to arrest what was nearly a child.

"I want everyone to keep their eyes open." Rucon didn't seem to like it either. "Report anything suspicious to me. And stay out of it. I don't need us getting caught up in a civil war."

Ria's com chimed and a woman's voice with a heavy southern accent said, "It's time to get a move on and load that shuttle, little missy."

"What, was that?" Rucon asked.

Ria snickered. "That's Harvey."

"It doesn't sound like a Harvey." Armond pursed his lips.

"Yeah well, he changes his gender. I never know what I'm going to get."

Mara laughed. "I think it's wonderful. Harvey is also correct. It's time to load the shuttles for our trip down to the surface."

Ria took one more look at the planet before they filed out of the room.

* * * *

Ty stood next to Merek on stage and waited while Father Arlo closed the curtains of the meeting hall. The muted light suited his mood, but he'd rather not be here at all. A certain fatalistic fog had descended upon him ever since watching Jafferies's murder. He wasn't a child any longer, and it was time Leon Jara was stopped. These meetings were useless.

Freckle-faced Connor jumped up to give the priest a hand before taking a seat next to Bella who sat with her legs dangling off the stage. The white-walled hall behind the church was standing room only, the younger teens standing on top of chairs and desks that had been pushed against the walls.

Two men came in from outside and approached Arlo. After a few words, they went back out and Arlo gave Merek a nod.

"All right everyone, time to settle down." The voices quieted, and all eyes turned to the stage. Merek cleared his throat. Everyone knew he hated speaking in front of such a large crowd, even though he'd known everyone here for years or even decades.

Ty crossed his arms. He scanned the room, taking in the faces of the men and women who formed this secret community. Curzans masquerading as Mitans and the occasional real Mitan mate. Word of the killing had spread fast and tension was high. Merek wanted to calm them down and get them refocused. "I'm sure you all know about Jafferies by now."

Murmurs and nods from the crowd.

"I don't have to tell any of you that the empire is changing."

"The empire is dead," a voice called out.

A few shouts of *"Hael!"* erupted.

Merek waved them quiet. "I also don't have to tell you things here on Mitah are getting critical."

From the back of the room, someone shouted, "Fracking Sandarians." This garnered a slew of reprimands, and from what Ty could tell, a mumbled apology by the offender. There were Mitans here after all. Unfortunately, the sentiment was a common one.

Merek spoke loud but un-rushed. "We have to remember not all Sandarians are our enemy. Look at Father Arlo here. Only those who seek to repress all things Curzan are our enemies."

"Only those with all the power, you mean," Connor hollered, and it garnered plenty of support.

"That's right," Ty spoke up. "And it's time for a change."

The crowd erupted again.

"And how do you suppose we do that?" someone called out.

Silence fell as they collectively waited for a reply. "One at a time," Ty said with determination.

Another eruption of voices and cheers.

Merek shot him a warning glance. "Ty, you're not helping."

"Ty's right," an older teen said. "We should deal with them one at a time, just like they do us. Jafferies won't be the last, you know."

That set the crowd off again.

"Oy!" Merek hollered. "Settle down. This is going to take time. We have to be smart, not rash."

They quieted to hear him out.

"You know we have people in government, plodding their way up." Merek let that sink in.

Heads nodded and people commented to each other.

Merek continued. "The Curzan underground across our planet is growing steadily every day. Trust us. The new mandate from the GTO decrees no more subjugation of non-psi beings."

Ty wanted to laugh. The GTO meant nothing here.

"Who cares?" said old Craggin near the front, echoing Ty's own thoughts. "Many of us aren't 'non-psi beings.' Never have been. And we ain't been nothin' but subjugated." He emphasized the last word and got a round of applause.

"I know, I know." Merek paced on the stage. "But as *you* know, no one outside of Mitah is aware of that. Now listen. We've been working on something. Something that could change everything, but let's face it. The GTO has its hands full right now. No one is going to care, not yet. But they will eventually. And when we find what we're looking for, we'll be ready for that day. It is coming."

"And what is this...thing?" Craggin eyed him suspiciously.

"Yeah, what are you talking about?" It was Connor who asked, and he was giving Ty a questioning look.

"I'm not at liberty to say." Merek looked uncomfortable. "But trust me, it will change everything. In the meantime, keep your ears open and your heads down because it's starting to look like the chancellor is getting inside information. No one knows how they found Jafferies or the others before him. We need to stick together. Anyone hears anything, let me know."

Ty fought to keep quiet. They were making progress with the texts, it was true, but Merek was putting too much faith into how much impact they would have. So what if they got their proof? Who were they going to take it to? No. The time for talk and texts was over. As soon as Merek wrapped up, Ty left out the side door. He needed to be alone. Needed to get his affairs in order. He didn't know if he would come through his encounter with Jara alive or not. And he didn't care as long as Jara was dead.

* * * *

Merek watched Ty make his escape from the church. Once the rest of the crowd dispersed, he sat on the edge of the stage with Bella and Father Arlo. "Our people are getting restless."

"And why not?" Arlo rubbed his temples. "Another killing. I fear that everything we've worked for is unraveling. The emperor is no more, but Chancellor Mortog is ever your executioner. Your people have the right to be restless."

Arlo Morton had taken over the church in Merek's hometown of Turin many years before. The priest had never treated Merek as anything other than an equal, even though he knew him to be Curzan. When Arlo's ten-year tenure was up, the church transferred him to Watersedge. In an unthinkable move, he'd smuggled Merek out with him and invented a background story. Merek set up shop as a Mitan woodworker and soon found his psi-mate, Trin.

Over the years, they had brought in Curzan refugees from all over Mitah. Backing each other's stories and histories, the community grew. They enjoyed the rights and perks of being Mitan, but lived in fear of discovery.

"Enough of this sad talk." Merek patted Bella on the back. "What of your work? How are you getting on with the texts?"

Bella kicked her heels against the stage side. "Every time we think we have something with one book, we aren't able to correlate it with the others."

"We have found similarities across the books," Arlo said, "but it's slow, tedious work. Thank the Goddess for Bella's young eyes."

Bella made a hissing sound. "You're not that old."

"Perhaps not," Arlo said, "but you're still much faster than me."

"That's not saying much." The teen smirked.

"Be polite," Merek said.

"I'm always polite."

Both men made sounds of disagreement, and the three of them shared a laugh.

"We need those texts deciphered," Merek said. "They're not only proof that Curzans had psi from the beginning, but they are part of our past. An entire history we know nothing about."

"We'll figure them out." Bella sobered. "Ty seemed pretty tense today."

Merek sighed deeply. "I shouldn't have let him stay to watch Jafferies die. I don't know what came over me. I couldn't pull myself away. He didn't need to see that, not after seeing his parents…"

"Don't blame yourself," Arlo said, placing a hand on his shoulder.

"It was my fault. He hasn't been the same since." He looked Arlo in the eyes. "I fear he's planning something foolish."

"What?" Both Arlo and Bella asked.

"The man who killed Jafferies, Leon Jara, also killed his parents."

Bella put a hand to her chest. "Mother Goddess. What do you think he's going to do?"

He could tell by her voice she knew exactly what Ty would do. He simply raised an eyebrow at her.

She looked away from him. "Do you really think he could do something like that?"

Merek shrugged. "He watched that man kill his folks. That demon has been riding his back for more than half his life."

"Couple that with his temper?" Arlo stood. "Chances are, we're going to have to save that boy."

Chapter 6

Ria hoisted her bag over her shoulder and followed the others out of the spaceport. Darl had sent open-air cruisers to pick them up. Rucon and Mara took one, along with the luggage, leaving Ria and the other EPs to take the second. It was a large vehicle with plenty of seats. Dani leaned into Ian's side on the front bench, leaving her and Armond with benches to themselves. Ria tossed her handbag into the back and crawled in after it.

They had made good time until they reached the outskirts of Watersedge where the cruiser slowed due to increasing traffic. The opening ceremonies of the ball were this evening, and people were streaming into town.

Ria was getting used to the phenomena of traffic on Earth but hadn't expected it here.

As if in response to her thought, the vehicle's AI spoke up. "Please be advised, we have obtained special dispensation to avoid the congestion. We will be diverting over the bay and the waters of the Marul Ocean if this is acceptable."

Ian responded in the affirmative and the cruiser lifted vertically, out of the line of traffic and veered off to the right. A few other vehicles performed similar maneuvers, but most remained in the increasing congestion.

This is more like it. Ria smiled as they soared over the ocean and then turned inland toward Watersedge. The town sat at the interior of a massive open-mouthed bay. Below the town, sheer cliffs dropped over three hundred feet to the ocean surface—a spectacular sight. The elevation tapered off near the mouth and white sand beaches stretched for miles on either side of the cliffs.

Every couple hundred yards or so massive staircases zigzagged down from the town to the water below. A suspended boardwalk with shops and restaurants had been cut right into the rock face near the water's surface. The bay provided a relatively calm harbor, and a bustling marina took up one end of the impressive landscape.

The water was light blue and surprisingly clear. Unlike Earth, which continued to consume dirty energy sources, Mitah had clean fuel, harvesting solar, wind, and tidal forces. It showed in everything from the sky to the ocean.

"Dani, check it out." Ria pointed to the ocean below.

Enormous ridged-backed creatures swam near the surface in a group. Ria counted sixteen before giving up. She snapped a picture with her com so she could research them later.

They were nearing the far side of town. Below, the streets were full of activity and the three miles of the Summer's Ball venue were clearly demarcated as pedestrian only. They soared over the streets, then into the mountains behind. The air smelled of forest as they landed at the front of a large, white stone estate. Vast lawns with perfectly trimmed gardens surrounded the place and butted up against the forest behind. An explosion of multicolored flowers covered the grounds. The smell was irresistible.

A swarm of servants were tending to the luggage when Rucon and Mara stepped out of their vehicle. They made a striking pair with Mara's small frame and jet-black hair against a red blouse, contrasting with Rucon's white shirt and blond locks. Ria filed out last and followed the others to meet their hosts.

Darl and his wife, Sherla, stood at the bottom of the steps that led to the entrance of their home. Pillars lined the front porch and two massive statues of some weird, long-legged animal sat on either side of the stairs, guarding the entrance.

It was a bit over the top for Ria's tastes but the overall effect was nice enough.

Where Rucon had stayed fit over the years, Darl was a bit on the soft side. His wife fit the image of a rich, powerful spouse. She was in a dress suit with blond hair perfectly styled and elegant jewelry that sparkled as she moved.

Ria stepped up at her turn and reached out to shake.

Darl surprised her with a kiss to the back of her hand. "And you must be Ria. Rucon told me about his team on Earth."

Ria waited for the comment on her size, but thankfully, it didn't come. She smiled, retrieved her hand, and turned to his wife.

Sherla shook her hand with a surprisingly firm grip. "It's nice to meet you, dear."

"I'd like to welcome all of you to our home," Sherla said. "Our staff will show you to your rooms. I've put you all in the same wing, which I hope is convenient. Please, make yourselves at home. We'll be having a light meal at six in the dining room before we go into town for the opening ceremonies. Feel free to come and go as you please during your stay. Simply ask one of our staff and a cruiser will be brought around for you. All you need to do is enter your destination and the autopilot will drop you off and park until you're ready for them to return."

Nice. Ria winked at Dani. They were both eager to get into the first of their new outfits. Abuzz with the anticipation and energy of all those in the town below, she followed the rest into the house, and they made their way to the guest suites.

A little over an hour later, Ria stood looking at her reflection. The opening ceremonies were all about fun. Attendees were encouraged to let their creativity soar and to dress in the spirit of the event. Ria selected a silver bodysuit made of shimmering fabric that fit perfectly and was accentuated with a jewel-encrusted belt. On top, she layered a floor length, nearly sheer shift of purple and green that flowed and fanned out when she moved. Patent leather knee-high boots gave her a four-inch boost in height. Bejeweled choker, earrings, and a matching headband completed her exotic look. Being back on Mitah had her thinking about Ty. They'd never exchanged numbers, and she didn't know if she'd be able to find his place. All she could do is hope for fate to jump in and lend a hand.

Dani knocked at her door, and the two headed downstairs to find they were the last to arrive. Mara came over, and the three gushed a mutual love-fest over each other's clothes.

The men stood gathered around the wet bar, decked out in suits of fantastical colors. Only Armond remained in EP attire.

"Wow," Ria said. "Way to be original, Armond."

Armond surveyed the other men. "Judging by these four, my attire will, in fact, be unique among the party goers."

Ria stuck her tongue out at him. He shook his head and returned to fiddling with the portal device.

Darl raised his glass to the ladies. "To the ravishing beauties in our midst."

Everyone toasted. Rucon leaned against the bar. "I was just about to ask our host to tell us a little more about the Curzan situation."

Darl used a wood tamper to press down the contents of an elaborately carved wooden pipe before puffing on the self-lighting bowl. "The whole business is starting to look quite sordid. It seems Chancellor Mortog is trying to keep it quiet, but word is spreading. After what I discovered last week, I believe it's true."

Rucon frowned. "The Curzan who was murdered?"

"Yes. It's extraordinary and highly disturbing. He's owned a small market at the edge of town for almost thirty years. Listed as Mitan, which implies he had psi."

Ria sat up straighter. "That would invalidate the Salvator's planetary rule. How is that possible?"

"We don't know. What we do know is that Anton Salvator has succumbed to a brain disease and Chancellor Mortog has been in charge for the past seven years. He's made no effort to hide his disdain of the natives."

"The PR, Salvator, has a son doesn't he?" Dani said. "Ian and I watched a few vids about Mitah."

"Yes, his name is Zander, but he's still at university. Has another year before taking his place."

"Which may not be his place if the rumors are true," Ria said.

"Correct." Darl frowned. "It could be worse than that. If Salvator's rule is deemed fraudulent, it might potentially undermine all land grants to us Mitans who have made this planet our home for generations. At very least, we deserve a tremendous amount of restitution, but I'm certainly not going to give up my lands. Curzans are considered to be of low intelligence and lacking in morals. They are barely above the status of animals here. It's quite complicated."

Ria blew out a breath and gazed among the well-lit gardens outside. "Sounds like Mitah is in for a wild ride."

* * * *

Ria spun around, arms wide, loving the way her shift floated around her. She understood why the Summer's Ball was such a popular event. A cool breeze blew in from the water. Music and laughter wafted through the night air that smelled of perfume and enticing foods. Multi-colored glowing orbs floated meters off the ground and strings of white lights were everywhere.

Darl had a table reserved not far from one of the many dance floors, within sight of one of the entertainment areas. The art museum was the hub of this area and stood atop a large hill between the lawns and mountains beyond. Three aerial dance troops wowed the crowds with stunning feats of synchronized airborne dance. They were dressed as ethereal-winged *Swali*.

"This is incredible." Ria had to shout to be heard over the music.

"Amazing," Dani agreed.

"Lord Rucon Cavacent, I presume?" a man's voice boomed.

Ria swung around to find Leon Jara and a shorter dark-haired man she recognized as Chancellor Mortog—de facto ruler of Mitah. He wore an ornate ceremonial robe with a heavy gold collar. He addressed Rucon, who stood to her left next to Mara.

Laric walked up behind his father and nodded to Ria, who decided to take the initiative. "Rucon, this is Leon Jara and his son, Laric. The Jaras were kind enough to host us when we came here to shop." The men shook hands, then Jara introduced everyone to the chancellor.

Ria took an instant dislike to the chancellor and was pretty sure she wasn't alone. He came across as one of those people who believed himself superior to everyone else.

"Jara tells me you moved your entire clan to Earth," Mortog said.

"Correct." Rucon crossed his arms and offered nothing further.

"That was a bold move. I've heard some other rumors as well. I haven't been able to verify them as yet, but I have been able to determine that the Portal Masters are behaving oddly. That makes me think the rumors must be true. Do you really have your own Portal Masters?"

Rucon held his stance. "I believe the Masters are men, not property."

Mortog frowned. "Of course. I didn't mean to insinuate—"

"As to the status of any Portal Masters," Rucon interrupted, "you'd have to ask them yourself."

Mortog's eyes squinted a fraction. "If there is anything I can do to make your stay here more…pleasant, be sure to let someone in my office know."

"I think we have everything sufficiently in order." Mara stepped closer and took Rucon's arm. "Come dear, dance with your wife."

The tension dissipated as Rucon and Mara drifted off.

Chancellor Mortog turned and left without a word, followed by Jara.

Laric glanced over his shoulder and shook his head. "Well, that was fun."

"The chancellor doesn't strike me as one to go out of his way for visitors," Ria said.

"He's not." Laric pulled at his chin. "He's certainly interested in those Portal Masters."

Ria shrugged. Rucon had hoped to keep the knowledge quiet but there was nothing to be done. "Care to show us around?"

"Sure." Laric held out his arm for Ria. "But first you have to meet my two half-siblings. They've been dying to meet off-worlders."

"Sounds good. How old are they again?"

"Joon and Leeda are ten. They're brats, but I'm rather fond of them."

"Lead the way then. Love your suit by the way."

Laric's suit shone with silver Mitah silk and had dark blue pinstripes that enhanced the perfect fit of the cut. Jara's table was only a few yards away from Darl's. The chancellor and Jara weren't in sight so they said their greetings to Nini and the twins. A boy and girl, they were beyond cute in little *Swali* costumes.

"You're the Earmot Protector, aren't you?" little Joon said. He was clearly the more outspoken of the two as Leeda seemed to have a deep fascination with the hem of her dress.

Ria smiled at the kids. "It's Earth, and yes, I am."

Joon used his foot and pushed a chair back. "Sit down, please. Laric said you'd tell me all about portals."

"And starships," Leeda added, not looking up.

Joon tilted his head sideways and rolled his eyes. "And starships. But portals first."

Leeda crossed her arms and pouted, but stayed silent.

Ria took the proffered chair. "Well, I don't have too much time but I can give you the short version of portal theory if you'd like."

"Yes please." Both children leaned closer, and Leeda looked up and smiled.

"Aside from the magic that Portal Masters use, which even I don't know about, there are limits which have to be obeyed. Other than that, it's pretty simple."

"What limits?" Joon asked.

"Well, you can only traverse a gateway four times in an hour with a maximum of about eight-hundred pounds each trip."

"If it's only eight-hundred pounds, how do you move starships?" Leeda was starting to find her voice.

"Good question," Ria said. "Starships are a bit different. They use interstellar jump points, which are a kind of portal, but you can't just fly from one to the other like walking through a gateway. You have to use special drives that are able to accelerate to incredible speeds and actually bend space and time. That bit of magic is done using a rare element called carnium, which we have on Earth."

"Whoa," Joon said looking totally transfixed. "That's cool."

"It is pretty cool," Ria said. She spent a few more minutes describing the Cavacents' transport ships before Laric rescued her.

"All right, you two. It's time I take this lady dancing."

"Aww," Joon said. "She hasn't told us about Earmot yet."

Ria laughed and didn't bother correcting him. "Next time, okay?"

"Promise?" Leeda asked.

Ria nodded. "Promise."

"They're adorable," Ria told Laric once they left. "And super smart."

"They are. Spoiled rotten, too."

"As they should be."

Ria spent the rest of the night dancing with Laric. It was a party like none other she'd experienced, and one she'd never forget.

* * * *

Ria existed as a point of light amongst the stars. Pure energy, she zipped from place to place, stopping momentarily, then zooming off to the next spot. Exhilaration and joy engulfed her as she explored her bodiless form. She traveled at the speed of light, and if she went fast enough, she could see her own trail and form a shape with light. She played with circles and rectangles, stars and swirls. She thrilled at the stops and starts needed to form the shapes. Pure joy engulfed her, and it was staggering.

She woke to the sound of her own laughter. She pondered the dream in the fog of a happiness hangover.

Okay, that was cool. "Harvey, what time is it?" She rolled to her side and reached for her com on the side table.

"It is nearly time for you to arise, madam." Harvey had taken on the personality of an English butler of late. "The crowds await to cheer you from the balcony."

"Very funny. Just tell me the time."

"The time is six twenty-eight in the morning of the forty-eighth day in the twenty-sixth year of the glory that was your creation, madam."

"Oy, no more birthday reminders," Ria said, swinging her legs off the plush mattress.

"As you wish, madam."

Ria eyed her com unit. She was kinda digging the whole butler thing. She stretched her arms and stood for a whole body routine, easing the sleep from her muscles. She flicked her hand, and the deep blue curtains slid aside, letting in the early morning sun. All the rooms in this wing faced Watersedge and the sea beyond. It was a calm day, and the sun glistened on the water. She thought back over the previous night. The opening ceremony for the Summer's Ball had been amazing. Watersedge went all out for the party. The master of ceremonies had kicked off the event with a live projection that was visible from every corner of the celebration. The costumes of the partygoers and the performers alike were magical and mystical. Everything about the event lent itself to a dreamlike state. Maybe that was why she'd had that dream. She smiled as a thrill shot through her at the memory of being a point of light. They'd stayed out late and indulged too much. This morning, she, Dani, and Ian were meeting Laric and going on a six-mile hike around Watersedge. That should clear the fog from her brain. She threw on some clothes suitable for a hike. Opening her bedroom door, the smell of something delicious drifted in, making her stomach growl. She decided to follow her nose when Dani and Ian emerged from their room down the hall.

Dani laughed at something he said as Ian playfully slapped her ass.

"All right you two, knock it off or go back to bed," Ria said.

Ian turned to go back inside, but Dani grabbed his arm. "No way. I'm starving. You smell that?"

He took a deep breath and nodded agreement. "All right. Food, then off to our hike. How'd you sleep, Ria?"

She thought of her dream and almost laughed out loud. "Heavenly. Did you two sleep at all?"

"Oh, stop," Dani said, smacking her on the arm.

Ria smacked her back. "You're just such a cute couple."

Ian frowned at her. "I don't do cute. Neither does Dani."

"Whatever," Ria said walking down the hall. "Come on. Time to eat."

Both Rucon and Darl were absent at breakfast. Mara sat with Sherla and an awkward-looking Armond.

Warming trays lined the length of the table along with breadbaskets and a large variety of fresh fruit, a number of which Ria didn't recognize.

"Good morning," Sherla said, motioning for the servant to add place settings to the table.

They exchanged greetings and dug into a fabulous breakfast.

"And what are your plans for this morning?" Sherla asked.

"We're meeting Laric Jara. He's taking us up the Range Wood trail," Ian said.

"Oh, that's lovely." Sherla plucked a small blue fruit from a bowl and slowly peeled it. "You do have repellers with you, yes?"

"Oh, yeah," Ria said. "We picked some up when we were here a month ago."

"Excellent." Sherla dropped a peel, revealing a juicy red interior.

Ria decided she would retrieve her dart before heading out, just in case. Laric assured her the repellers were sufficient to keep the dangerous animals away, but she'd feel better with an actual weapon. She pulled her com from her pocket. "Harvey, can you show me a vid and a brief on a local animal called a worick?"

"It would be my immense pleasure, madam," her com replied.

Sherla giggled. "Mara told me about Harvey. You are a clever girl, aren't you Ria."

Dani gave her a little push. "Clever girl. You'd make a great companion for The Doctor."

One of Ria's favorite TV shows on Earth was Doctor Who. "That I would." She pulled up the holo of the worick for all to see. "That's one nasty beastie."

Harvey screamed like a teenage girl, and Ria nearly dropped it. "Again? What the *frack*, Harvey. Never do that again. Ever."

"My apologies, madam. I felt it an appropriate response to the creatures in this vid."

"Yeah, well, it's not. Just stick to the butler persona, okay?"

"Yes, madam."

The vid showed a pack of five woricks. Four legged, they moved like lions. Their bone structure was clearly visible underneath leathery skin. Bony-looking spikes protruded along their spines. They stood three to four feet at the shoulder, and their heads bore the shape of a chevron. The top two-thirds of their head consisted of the same bony substance as their backs. Their eyes were wide set, and the bottom third of their head was all mouth, filled with sharply pointed teeth. Four-inch claws on muscular legs made for a terrifying sight.

"They say those jaws can snap a body in half with one bite." Sherla sunk her teeth into a slice of the fruit, red juice dripping down her chin.

Ria shivered and put Harvey away.

* * * *

It was the second night of the Summer's Ball, and Ria was back with the others, ready for a magic-filled evening. The hike that morning had been just what they needed to get ready for another night of fun. The forest was beautiful and refreshingly cool under the cover of the evergreens.

Tonight, the women sported wings and everyone wore masks. The wings were glossy transparent creations that moved with the breeze. There was disagreement among the locals whether or not the *Swali* were real or mythical, but either way, they made fun inspiration for costumes. Women with similar winged gowns drifted and danced everywhere. The music had the same hauntingly beautiful feel as the night before, and dimly lit globes of pink, purple, green and blue hovered around the vast expanse of the museum grounds.

Ria decided that the tables Darl reserved were in a great location with easy access to food and drink, as well as dancing.

"I want you kids to make the most of this," Darl said, slightly slurring his words. "Not everyone gets to see the glory of our Summer's Ball." He'd already had a fair amount to drink, and Ria suspected he wouldn't last the night.

"He's right you know," Sherla chimed in. "You must start tonight with a walk to the top of the stairs of the museum. I believe you missed it last night, yes?" She pointed to the centerpiece of the vast lawns they occupied. The white-columned building was alight with multicolored floodlights adding to the fairy-tale effect.

"The porch goes all the way around," Sherla continued, "and we are fairly near the center of the festivities. These lights"—she motioned to the hovering globes—"demarcate the extent of the ball. It's a beautiful sight up there."

"Gotta see that," Ria said, getting to her feet. "You guys up for it?"

All the EPs went, even Armond who seldom appeared to enjoy himself. Rucon and Mara stayed behind with Darl and his wife.

"No peeking on the way up," Sherla called out after them.

Armond and Ian led the way with the girls following behind. Ria managed not to look around until they reached the top. The sight took her breath away. There must have been tens of thousands of lights spanning the three-mile area, all casting a faint glow on the town.

"Wow," Ria said.

They made their way around the building, weaving in and out of other people enjoying the sight.

"I like this view best," Ria said, stopping where they'd come up.

Beyond the lights, the mountains rose in the distance. The ball occurred during the double full moons and the mountains glowed with an eerie light. Ria shivered even though the night was a bit on the warm side.

"I don't know," Dani said. "I think I might like the ocean view over the cliffs more. Look how they reflect the lights."

Ria turned to the east. "It might be a tie."

Ria made her way back down the steps of the museum with the others, stopping for some drinks along the way. The music now was lively and perfect for dancing.

They reached their table and Ria set down her drink. "Dani, come dance with me." She spun in a circle and made a sweeping gesture with her arm. "We will be *Swali* together and fly to the stars."

* * * *

With his brightly colored mask, Ty blended in with the crowds as he wove his way toward Jara's table. The sun had set and the dual moons overhead cast their glow across the partygoers. Music, the sounds of laughter, and people talking loudly drifted through the night air. This was the first Summer's Ball since the fall of the empire and the energy was different. There were more off-worlders than ever before, and the crowds were thick in the center of the festivities.

A couple holding hands jostled him as they made their way to the dancing area. The man took the *Swali* in his arms and kissed her deeply before they began to sway and gyrate together. Too close and too slow for the upbeat music.

Ty clenched his fists and moved on, scanning the crowd. His body tensed.

Leon Jara stood at the edge of the dancers, facing away, speaking to an older man. Jara's posture screamed military discipline.

Reaching into his pocket Ty fingered the small, but deadly, laser. It brought no comfort. He made his way closer, heart beating faster with every step. A bead of sweat trailed down his temple. This was the man who killed his parents, old Jafferies, and Goddess only knew how many more Curzans. When he came within earshot of Leon, he stopped and listened.

"...they're ten. Yes, this is their first ball. Very excited. The nanny has taken them back to our lodgings for the night."

He has a family. Ty squeezed his eyes closed. *Children.* How could he do to those kids what their father had done to him? A lifetime of pain and longing. *I can't do this.* He flung his mask to the ground and turned to leave when someone grabbed his arm in a painful grip.

Ty stared into the eyes of the devil himself.

Leon had an iron hold on him. "I know you, boy." He looked at Ty with absolute loathing. "What do you think you're doing here, heh?" He leaned in and spoke into Ty's ear so no one else could hear. "You're on my list, did you know that? You and those Sordinas. I'm going to enjoy ridding our planet of your scum."

Ty tried to pull away, but Leon wasn't letting go.

"But not Bella. No, not Bella. I'm going to take my time with that one."

Ty held the murderer's gaze, pulled out the laser, and sliced a path from his stomach to underneath his chin.

A look of shock crossed Jara's face before he crumpled to the ground.

* * * *

Ria flung her arms wide and let the music move her. As she approached the edge of the dance floor, a familiar buzz started from her core. *Ty.* Something was wrong. She eagerly looked around, trying to find him. When she did, she froze. "Oh, Goddess."

"What's wrong?" Dani followed her gaze.

"Get Ian!" Ria bolted for Jara, but it was too late.

Screams echoed through the crowd. Jara's wife rushed to his side as Ty turned and ran.

Ria was almost on him, so she gathered her psi and slammed Ty to the ground. More people screamed and panicked as they realized what had happened.

Ria stood, feet planted apart, keeping Ty pinned with her psi. The connection made her buzz, but it was horrible and confused. Not like before. Rage and sadness and a dozen other emotions poured into her. And pleasure. It was sick.

Head on the ground, Ty hollered. The sound reverberated deep inside, and she caught her breath. She nearly let go before Ian and Armond arrived. Staggering back, she let them take over. She stood shaking as Ian pulled a band from an inside pocket of his jacket and bound Ty's wrists.

Once they had him secured, they hoisted him to his feet, keeping a firm grip.

When he met her gaze, hatred, pure and simple, rolled off him. Hatred directed at her. *What the frack?* A storm of emotion blasted her. Their intense attraction battled with his emotions. Clenching her fists, she stepped closer to him. "What have you done, Ty?" It came out with more force than she intended.

Dani stood next to her, and Ian and Armond shot her a questioning look. "You know him?" Ian asked.

Ria was barely keeping it together. The intensity of their connection made her feel like her mind was splitting. She grabbed her head and squeezed. "Why did you do that?"

"What is going on here?" A man's voice broke through her fog.

She turned to find a thin-framed man with greasy hair. He wore a uniform she recognized as Mitah security. He had an air of authority and appeared to be in charge. Others in similar uniforms filed in and started clearing the scene of onlookers. In the immediate area, the globes of colored light turned white and formed a circle. A moment later, the air between the globes shimmered and an opaque wall surrounded the group. The sound was muted and the light had an eerie, ethereal quality to it.

"I'm Lieutenant Sou, and someone better start talking before I have you all arrested."

"He killed the man over there." Ian motioned to Jara's body.

The sound of Nini's wailing reverberated around the small space.

"Someone shut her up," Sou said.

One of the officers approached Sou and spoke in his ear.

"Jara? Are you sure?"

The man nodded before leaving them.

"Well that's just perfect, isn't it? Not only do we have a dead body, but it's the chancellor's new favorite." The smirk on Sou's face made him look almost pleased.

Ria's control started slipping again. "Tell me why, Ty?"

Ty shot her a look of pure malice. "I don't have to tell you anything." His voice was so low she almost missed it.

"You know this Curzan?" Sou asked.

Ria clenched her fists. "Yes. No. I—wait, Curzan?"

Sou looked between Ria and Ty. "Yes, Curzan. He was to be rounded up next week for impersonating a Mitan. There's a whole lot of 'em getting ready to pay for their crimes."

Sou called out to his men who took Ty from Ian and Armond. For some reason, they placed an additional set of bands on his wrists. The moment the bands were in place the intense barrage of emotion from his psi stopped.

Ria took a shaky breath. The absence was both a relief and a pain. "What do you mean he's Curzan? I thought they didn't have psi. That man has psi."

"And exactly how do you know this?"

Sou was making her uncomfortable and angry.

There was a commotion beyond the perimeter. Laric's voice could be heard arguing with someone on the outside.

"Let him in," Ria said to Sou.

"Are you giving me orders now?"

Ian stepped next to her before she could give the lieutenant a special kind of order. "Easy, Ria. This is their planet. We have no authority here."

She motioned to the body. "The man making all the noise out there is Leon Jara's son. He's a friend."

Sou nodded to one of the officers, and Laric stepped through.

Ria moved to go to him but Sou stopped her. "Hold on. I'm not done with you yet."

The look of devastation on Laric's face as he knelt down next to Leon was heartbreaking. He wrapped an arm around Nini who'd gone silent and was clearly in shock. One of the men with Sou was scanning the body with a recording device. A group of medics with a hover stretcher waited nearby. No one seemed to know what to do with the two grievers nearby.

Ria swung back to Ty. After their intense connection, it was like he wasn't there. All she had were her own emotions, which were seriously messed up. She couldn't sense anything from him. She guessed it had something to do with the extra set of bands on his wrists. Just as well, given the effect he had on her.

Ian reached a hand out to Sou. "We're the protectorate team for a planet called Earth."

"So I heard." Sou looked around the scene with distaste. "This is only the second time we've had a murder at the Summer's Ball. Chancellor isn't going to like it. Now, someone want to tell me what exactly happened?"

"You'll have to ask Ria. She had him down before we arrived."

"That so?"

Ria bristled at his tone. "Yes. That's so."

Sou eyed her from top to bottom, his skepticism obvious. "Well? Let's hear it then."

"All I saw were the last few moments. Leon had a hold of his arm. The man had a laser blade and…and I wasn't fast enough. He slit him from stomach to head." Ria looked at Ty, not able to comprehend why he would do it. Her anger stirred. "Leon has two young children. Did you know that, Ty?"

He wouldn't respond. Just stared at the ground a few feet ahead.

Ria wanted to grab hold and shake him till he answered her. "Did you know that?" she yelled.

His head snapped up, and he stared at her. She sensed his emotions but it was devoid of psi, which was a bizarre sensation for her. His anger was nearly psychotic.

"You better get him out of here," she said. "He's getting ready to snap."

"Not with our bands on him," the Lieutenant said. "That one of your abilities? Reading emotions?"

"Yes." Ria resented having to answer the man.

Sou eyed her a long moment. "Just so we're clear. You know Leon and his son there, and you know the killer?"

"Yes."

"How do you know Leon?" He looked skeptical.

"I did my military training with Laric. We stayed with them when we were here shopping." Pain stabbed at her when she thought of Laric.

Ty's head tilted slightly, and his anger intensified.

Ria shook her head. *Are you insane? Is that it?*

"And how do you know this Curzan?"

Ria flashed back to her night with Ty. He'd dropped his gaze back to the ground, but she knew he was remembering as well. "We went on a date when Dani and I were here last. That's all. One date. I haven't seen or talked to him since that night."

Sou eyed her critically, again scanning her body head to toe. "You went on a date with a Curzan?"

"I didn't know he was a Curzan. You said yourself he was impersonating a Mitan."

Sou grunted. "Well, you're not to leave Mitah until I can look into this further."

"Sir, with all respect, I tried to save Jara and captured the killer."

"That don't mean there isn't more to the story here. Where are you staying?"

Ria wanted to tell him it was none of his business, but Ian's voice stopped her.

"Let it go. We need to cooperate with the locals. Tell him what he wants to know." Unlike most, Ian was strong enough to project his thoughts.

Ria couldn't answer, but his intent was loud and clear. She took a calming breath. "We're staying with the Kartons."

"That be Darl Karton? Up on the hill there?" Sou nodded toward the mountains that towered to the west.

"Yeah, up on the hill."

In the end, he insisted on questioning the rest of the team and verifying they were, in fact, staying with the Kartons.

Ria was sure he was deliberately dragging things out. He finally let them go, and she was able to grab a few minutes with Laric before they took away his father's body.

It made her sick. If only she'd gotten to him sooner. How could Ty do that?

Once the space had been cleared and cleaned, the lights reassumed their bright colors and the wall disappeared. The guards escorted Ty away without incident. Outside their bubble, the ball had carried on as though nothing had happened.

She watched Ty's back disappear into the crowds. People laughing and dancing replaced his departing form. There was a major disconnect between what she saw and how she felt. Part of her couldn't believe the man that had brought her so much pleasure was such a brutal killer. It didn't fit.

Dani took her hand and gave it a squeeze. "I think we're done for tonight."

Ria nodded and followed the others. She thought of Laric and his half-siblings. She thought of Ty and her connection with him. He was a Curzan and a killer.

Watersedge was ablaze in colored lights as they flew over the festivities in the cruiser on the way back to the Kartons. It was beautiful and so very sad.

Chapter 7

Loc Zorton stood in the inner sanctum of the Portal Masters' Guild on Sandaria. Deep underground, the ancient walls of roughly carved-out mertoc rock stood sentinel over the center of the room where a large object radiated a deep red glow. Gas-fed torches lined the walls, providing the only source of light. Inside the smooth stone-like surface lived the heart of the guild's power—the key to their ability to create interstellar portals, a secret known only to a few. Loc's short term as head of the guild had been tenuous at best, but he felt he was making progress. Now, however, old Merrin was up to something. His gnarled fingers tapped on the surface of the wood table and his black guild robes smelled of smoke.

Loc usually liked this cool, dark space, but not today. "You must be mistaken. We all know you can't create a portal with only one end. Something has to anchor it. Basic theory." It was clear from the look on their faces that they knew something he didn't. Merrin loved his games and mysteries.

"What aren't you telling me?" Loc crossed his arms, enjoying the weight of the hand-stitched robes worn only by the head of the guild.

Merrin smiled over his steepled fingers. "He had an anchor."

"Of course, he had an anchor. A second device, as always."

Merrin shook his head slowly. Loc waited until it was clear the old Portal Master was going to make him ask for it. "What then?" he said through gritted teeth.

"Our own portal." Merrin pulled out his com and projected a holo display. It showed the standard waveform of an active portal on Sandaria. Old data, it wasn't live. "We know when Armond ported Rucon's EPs away from Gordat Prayda, it was here." He pointed to a slight phase shift in the waveform. The signature was what the Torogs used to track down the devices from Vertan. Devices that allowed Vertans to create interstellar portals of their own. They'd discovered the planet almost thirty years ago. The Vertans had been exploring the stars for only a few decades and had gone out of their way to remain undetected by the empire. They were mere children among the stars. Abilities such as theirs were not easily hidden, and once the guild found out, they moved quickly. With the help of Torogs, the planet was quarantined, their space-faring capabilities removed, and a prolonged mission to apprehend all portal-making devices was launched. Very few knew of the existence of the planet, and even fewer their ability to create portals.

Merrin studied Loc's face, allowing time for the information to sink in. "Within the next minute, Rucon himself was ported directly to Earth."

"We already know this," Loc said.

"Yes, but what we failed to notice was this." The data on the holo blinked out and was replaced by a new set. Loc took a closer look. "Those are the portals on Earth. So?"

Merrin used his psi and created two vertical lines in the graph display. "This is the time frame Rucon ported out."

"That's the normal signature for one of our portal moves."

"Correct."

Loc was starting to see where this was going, and he didn't like it. "You're saying that wasn't one of us?"

"Now you see."

"He used a Vertan device on one end and our own portal to anchor?" Loc shook his head. "Surely, we would have discovered it by now if that were possible."

The old man shrugged. "The Vertans could easily hide such a thing from us. Or perhaps they don't know they can do it themselves."

"We can't let word of this get out. They could create portals across the galaxy anywhere ours exist. That would be our undoing."

"Agreed. The fact that they have yet to do so makes me think they are unaware of the possibility, or perhaps there is something else going on. Regardless, given our lack of full Masters, we must find a solution."

"I suppose you have one?" Loc resented having to ask, and Merrin knew it. The old man had nearly won Loc's position as head of the guild and made no effort to hide his animosity.

"I do. Until now, we have used our abilities to alter their devices in the only way possible. To send them back to their own planet. But what if we were able to bring them someplace else? Someplace like here, perhaps."

Loc tilted his head. "We don't have that ability."

"We don't. No." Merrin leaned back in the chair and crossed his arms. "But they do."

Loc thought a moment and came to the only conclusion. "You want to bring Vertans here and use them to create portals for us." *Slavery.* He almost said it aloud, but he didn't. It was instantly clear that the plan would work. They could go on making portals and the GTO would know nothing. It was a good idea. "They could never leave Sandaria."

"Correct." Merrin's thin lips pressed into what passed for a smile.

"I believe your pet Torogs could assist in rounding them up."

"They could."

Loc was certain the old man had already implemented the plan, but he didn't need to advertise his disregard for Loc's command.

"I regret that this is necessary," Loc said, "but in order to save our guild, I believe it is our only choice. Have the Torogs track down twelve Vertans. Bring them here immediately upon capture. I suspect it will take some convincing to get them to cooperate."

"If I were you, Loc, I'd be more concerned with what we're going to do if the GTO discovers we've had an entire planet under quarantine for nearly thirty years."

"Do you think one second *ever* goes by without that weighing on me?"

"I should hope not."

Loc spun around and left the chamber. Merrin was right, of course. It was how they were maintaining their power. The planet of Sandaria, although beautiful, had no natural resources to speak of. The reason for its affluence was the Portal Masters. Planets paid dearly for the creation of portals and continued paying in order to maintain them. Limitations inherent in portals would mean interstellar ships would always be necessary, but having one or more portals on a planet was a sign of great prestige. Vertan and its people must be contained at all cost.

* * * *

Ria's heart pounded as she ran into the forest. The tall trees helped with the rain, but large drops still pelted her face. Night had fully fallen, and the wet ground slowed her progress. She stumbled over an exposed tree root. Frack.

Branches scraped across her arms and face. Someone was in front of her. Someone on her side. Muffled footfalls and angry curses of their pursuers followed from behind. Farther to their left came the frenzied sound of woricks barking. Fear ripped through her, but she pushed it aside.

"Faster. We have to go faster." She didn't know who she spoke to.

They stepped up the pace. The mountain loomed overhead on their right. The ground rose to a punishing incline. Her legs and lungs burned. They'd run for so long her psi was drained. She wouldn't last much longer. Still, they pushed on.

Die now or die later. We have to keep going.

They reached the base of the cliffs and veered left. It was open here. Exposed. The relentless rain battered them. They searched for something. Ria slipped on the wet rocks and fell, smashing her knee into a sharp edge. She stifled a cry. A firm hand gripped her arm and helped her up. Who was she with? She couldn't see a face. They continued along the base of the mountain.

There!

Ahead was a fissure in the rock. They approached quickly, but with caution. Ria glanced back. The forest was dense below, and she couldn't see anything, but the men's voices and the barking grew louder. They would breach the forest any second. Rain poured down her face.

Whoever she was with disappeared into the side of the mountain. She took a deep breath and followed. A narrow space. Jagged stone scratched her arm, tearing into the wounds left by the trees below. She bit back a cry. It was cold here. Her stomach knotted in terror, and she wanted to scream.

Water poured in from above. The fissure went all the way to the top. She wiped the water from her eyes and blinked, trying to see. I've been here before.

Deeper they went.

Why was this happening? Who was after them? Why did she have to be with this person? Because somehow she knew she did have to be with him. She fought back tears of frustration and fear.

She moved her gaze to the man ahead of her and stared into steel gray eyes. A look of horror dawned on his face as a laser pierced her side from behind.

Ria bolted upright in bed and checked her side for injury. Her heart pounded, and the fear was far too real. She blew out a breath.

Ty. She had to focus on breathing slow. An emotion so strong it bordered on pain tore through her. No. It couldn't be.

This was the third time she'd had the dream, but she'd never been able to see who was with her. Till now. Flipping back the damp sheets, she swung her legs off the bed and stretched her arms up and back.

Three days had passed since Leon Jara's death. The others had returned to Earth, but she remained, waiting for Lieutenant Sou to approve her departure. He didn't know the portal existed. She could leave at any time, but Rucon wanted her to abide by the rules. They were strict rules, too. They'd tagged her DNA and would know if she left the planet. Which totally sucked because she couldn't even use the sim arena back on Earth. Her exercise was limited to hiking the surrounding forests and beaches and lifting weights. Not nearly as effective or exhilarating as battling it out in a sim. She was antsy, needed to exercise. Ty's gray eyes rose in her mind. He'd seen her just now. She felt the psi connection but refused to connect the dots. *Relax, it's just a dream.*

Dropping her arms, she stood and headed for the shower. Lieutenant Sou would be here in under an hour. She was pretty sure he had ulterior motives for keeping her on Mitah.

After showering, she dressed quickly and put on her hiking boots.

"If you please, madam." Harvey spoke up with his clipped British accent. "Miss Dani is hailing you."

"Thank you, Harvey. Put her through."

"Morning." Dani sounded disgustingly happy as usual.

"Morning, Sunshine. Everything okay on Earth?"

"Kind of boring, actually. Any news yet?"

"No." Ria sighed. "Do you think you could have Ian talk to Rucon? Maybe he can pull some strings. I want to get out of here, but before I do, I need to see Ty." The words were out of her mouth before she had even processed the thought. Her body buzzed with a foreign energy at the idea of being near him.

"What? Why?"

Ria didn't know how to answer. It was a good question. What did she think would happen? *He's a cold-blooded killer.*

"Ria?"

"I'm here. I just… I don't know what to say, Dani. I need to see him. Alone." *What the frack? Where am I going with this?*

"Alone? What aren't you telling me? You know what? Never mind. I'm coming over." Dani and Ian stepped through the portal less than ten minutes later.

Ian didn't beat around the bush. "Tell us exactly why you want to see him alone?"

Dani sucked in her breath. "It's the dreams, isn't it?"

She'd confided in Dani after the second dream. They felt so real, so final. Ria didn't want to say it out loud, but there was no getting around it. "I saw who it was this morning. It's Ty."

"What do you mean?" Ian said, looking back and forth between the two women.

Ria told him about the dreams. "I have this horrible feeling that he's my psi-mate. Why else would this be happening? The night I went out with him…" Ria rubbed her face. "I thought it was just great chemistry, but I saw him this time Ian. I saw him, and he saw me. I think my psi-mate is a killer."

Ian stayed silent for a long moment, no doubt sorting through the implications. "Ria, I'm sorry, but what do you expect is going to happen, even if we can get you in to see him?"

"I don't know. Maybe I'm wrong. I really need to be wrong, Ian. Just do it, okay?"

* * * *

Rucon Cavacent was back on his transport ship. He stood by the bar in the observation room, drumming his fingers on the polished wood. He could easily have used the portal to get to Mitah, but he didn't want to tip his hand. No one knew they had the ability to create portals, and he wanted to keep it that way.

Lieutenant Sou waited for him planet-side. The man's stringy light brown hair needed washing. "It's good to see you again, Mr. Cavacent."

"It's Lord Cavacent." Rucon wiped the man's sweat from his palm. Ian and Dani implored him to come and see to Ria's release along with what he thought to be a very strange request. The chancellor had been more than happy to meet with him, and Rucon sincerely hoped he didn't bring up the Portal Masters again.

Sou accompanied him in the cruiser through the city to the planetary ruler's Palace. Mortog wasn't the PR, but he might as well have been. Until the PR's son, Zander, came to power in little over a year, Mortog was the one in charge.

The palace wasn't lacking in opulence. Artwork and sculptures adorned every space. Sou, who was obviously at home here, showed Rucon to a comfortable room off the main foyer.

"I'll let the chancellor know you're here," Sou said, bowing awkwardly and departing.

Bay windows overlooked a manicured lawn and well-tended gardens. Rucon paced. He should be back on Earth, overseeing the construction of the new compound, not here placating local law enforcement. He'd spoken with Ria earlier and, aside from daily visits by Sou, she was left to her own devices. It didn't make sense to keep her any longer.

Rucon's impatience was nearing its limit when Chancellor Mortog finally appeared. The robes he'd worn to the ball were absent. The man was leaner and more fit than Rucon had realized. Sou hovered in the background like a dog worshiping his master.

"Lord Cavacent." Mortog held out his hand. "So good to see you again."

"Chancellor. I'm sure you know why I'm here." Rucon didn't see the need for unnecessary pleasantries.

"I believe so. Lieutenant Sou informs me we have one of your Protectors. A Miss Montori, was it?"

A faint twinge tickled the back of Rucon's mind. "That is correct. She has a job to do, and unless you have reason to keep her, we'd like her back."

Sou looked pathetic, and Rucon suspected Ria had been correct about his motivations being less than professional.

"Lieutenant?" Mortog said.

Sou straightened his shirt. "I suppose we've got everything we need from her."

"Good." Rucon didn't wait for anything further. "I have one more request. She'd like to see Jara's killer."

"That's a highly unusual request, Lord Cavacent." Sou squirmed and wrung his hands.

Rucon wanted to scratch the back of his head, but the increasingly odd sensation wasn't external. "I agree it is unusual, but given the inconvenience you've caused us perhaps you could see to it."

Mortog kept his eyes on Rucon but nodded in Sou's direction.

The smaller man's shoulders dropped a fraction. "I guess I could oversee that," Sou said.

"One more thing," Rucon said. "She will see him alone." He felt the twinge again and saw a slight tick around Mortog's left eye.

"Are you quite sure about that?" Mortog asked.

"I am."

The color in the chancellor's face rose slightly before he waved at Sou. "See that it is done."

The little man looked shocked, but said nothing.

Rucon's com notified him of an incoming communication. He directed it to take the call and hold. "I believe I'm done here, then. Good day."

It was obvious that Mortog wasn't happy with the way the meeting had transpired and simply nodded as Rucon departed. Once he was outside the building, he answered the call. "Yes?"

"Is this Lord Cavacent?"

"It is."

"Good. My name is Zander Salvator. Do you have a moment to meet?"

It took Rucon a moment to place the name. Salvator was the name of the planetary ruler's family. "Are you the PR's son?"

"I am."

He had nothing else to do and was curious about the boy. "I can meet you now if you'd like." Rucon followed directions to the residential quarters of the palace. An elderly man in servant's attire greeted him at the door. The man bowed low, then led the way. They walked down a wide corridor, the walls covered in life-size portraits of the planetary rulers. Glistening marble and gold brocade were everywhere. Large windows kept the space from being oppressive.

The servant came to a set of double doors and knocked once before entering the study. A handsome boy with wavy blond hair rose to greet him. He was tall and muscular but hardly looked the twenty-two years he was reported to be.

"Lord Cavacent?"

Rucon extended his hand. "Please, call me Rucon."

"In that case, you may call me Zander."

The men sat facing each other in plush chairs while the servant brought in a caff service.

Rucon glanced over Zander's head to the portrait that hung over the fireplace. "Is that your father?"

Zander didn't turn to see what Rucon referenced. "Yes. That was done shortly before...well, I'm sure you've heard the story by now."

"Degenerative brain disease. I am sorry." He wanted to ask if they were certain there was no cure, but surely they would have exhausted the possibilities.

Zander took a drink and set his cup down. "I'm told you were just meeting with Chancellor Mortog?"

"Correct. He, or perhaps more accurately his Lieutenant Sou, is holding one of my protectors. I assume you heard of Leon Jara's murder?"

Zander's knee bounced. "Only just recently. They said your protectors captured him and that this Ria Montori of yours witnessed the event."

"She did more than witness it. She apprehended him." Rucon took a drink of his caff. Saying it out loud had him wondering if that had something to do with her desire to see the boy alone.

Zander appeared to be weighing something. Finally, he stood and stared into the empty fireplace before turning to Rucon. "I have been away from my home for too long and yet still have the final year at university before I am of age and can take my father's place."

"I am aware of your situation."

"Chancellor Mortog has not been forthcoming with me. I requested to be present when he met with you. I will see to it that Ms. Montori is released. There are other channels available to me outside the chancellor and his pets."

The underlying message of discord in the planet's rule was loud and clear to Rucon. "I believe the situation has been dealt with. However, I appreciate your concern."

A knock at the door interrupted them. A tall dark-haired woman in a long, azure dress stood in the doorway. She had been a beauty once, but now her face was drawn and sallow. She had the vacant look of a shell-shocked soldier. "I'm sorry, dear. I didn't know you had a visitor. I'll come back later."

"Mother, wait," Zander said, going to her. "I'd like you to meet someone. He's the one I told you about. He has the protectorship of a planet called Earth. The Empire—well, the GTO now—gets a great deal of their carnium from there. Sou has been detaining one of his people. Do you remember?"

The woman looked confused, but answered properly. "Yes, of course."

"Rucon, this is my mother, Mariah Salvator."

Rucon went to her and kissed the back of her hand. "It is an honor to meet you."

"And you." She bowed her head. "We used to travel off-world, my husband and I." Her gaze shifted to the windows behind Zander's desk. "They tell me the emperor is no longer." Turning to Zander she said, "It will be so nice when you're home for good." She placed her hand on his cheek, then left without another word.

Zander watched her go, his shoulders dropping slightly. "I'm sorry. She's been like this for the past year. The further away my father gets, the more she withdraws." The boy sighed. "You would have liked her. She brought laughter wherever she went."

Rucon tried to hide his shock. Zander had effectively lost both parents. "Is she...like your father?"

"The doctors say she's fine. They love each other very much. I have hope she'll come back to herself someday."

Rucon pictured the woman's eyes. There was something more than just grief in their depths. He said his goodbyes to Zander and left for his ship where he was staying. He thought back to the boy and the pain he must be experiencing. And to Mortog. There was something off about that man. *This isn't my planet. These aren't my problems.* He repeated the phrase to himself as he left. He'd collect Ria once she'd had her meeting, and they would leave it all behind.

* * * *

Ty came to his senses slowly. His lower lip pulsed, and his right eye refused to open. The straps keeping him upright dug into his arms and below his ribs. He blinked repeatedly, trying to get his one eye to focus.

"Look who's back for more." The image before him cleared. He'd seen this man before. Short, balding, with a high-pitched voice. He enjoyed the beatings more than any of the others. He held a bucket and grinned before dousing Ty.

The shock of cold water cleared his head some, but the shivering started again. The cell had metal walls and a drain in the concrete floor. A metal table against one wall, a small sink and the rack that held him restrained in a vertical position. Cozy. Two lamps stood facing him, and bright lights shone from the ceiling above.

Ty met the man's gaze.

"Time you start talking, boy. Chancellor wants names of those in your little underground, and I'm going to be the one to give 'em to him."

He picked up a short leather strap and lashed out with precision. He'd been working that set of ribs for days.

The smell of leather, blood, sweat, and Gods only knew what else made Ty sick. He gritted his teeth. The bands that held him were something new. He couldn't fathom how they worked, but they made it so his psi couldn't extend beyond his body. After the first six or seven hours, the pain had morphed into something different. He didn't feel it so much as he'd become the pain. With each strike, the agony had combined with his captive psi and defined itself into a separate entity. This alternate existence was more real now than his body. Ty could only hope there was no permanent damage. The thought nearly made him laugh. Last time he checked, dying was pretty permanent. He struggled to hold onto consciousness, but knew he'd faded in and out when memories of the moments prior couldn't be true.

He'd just been in the mountains overlooking Watersedge, but that wasn't possible. He was here. In the Starfall jail. *Focus.*

A loud reedy voice pulled him from his thoughts. "Let him down and clean him up."

Lieutenant Sou.

"He's going to have a visitor tomorrow. Get Mortog's healers in here and make him pretty."

The door slammed.

Baldy grumbled something about interrupting his art before releasing Ty. The band at his chest fell away. His body swung forward. Baldy freed his wrists next. He dropped to his knees and fell over sideways, his arms numb and useless to break his fall.

His head smashed into the floor...

And he was running.

Sou and his henchmen were coming after them. They broke the cover of the trees and ran along the base of the cliff. Where was he? Rain pelted his face, and the smell of the forest, fresh and clean, filled his lungs. They were close. He wanted to look back, see who was with him, but they couldn't slow down. The entrance was just ahead. A stifled cry came from behind. He turned.

A woman with red hair plastered to her face. Ria.

He became disembodied from the dream and watched as he grabbed her arm and helped her up. Anger washed over him. Why was he helping her?

He held her tight as they stumbled forward. The vertical crevice ahead was the key. So close. He entered first, making sure they were alone. He didn't think a worick would fit in here but had to be sure. Ty wanted to make himself stop. He shouldn't be helping her.

She cried out, and he turned to face her.

Green eyes bore into him.

Why would I help a military crag? Anger shook him. She was Sandarian military. They kill Curzans. He wanted to kill her, not help her. Then he saw the blood pouring from the wound at her side. Grief tore through him, and he bellowed out his pain.

He lashed out only to find his hands bound to a small cot.

Standing over him was Lieutenant Sou. They were in a different room. Small, whitewashed walls and a sink and toilet. A standard cell in the Starfall jail. Not his usual accommodation. He must have been out for a while. He tested the restraints. He couldn't move, but his body wasn't wracked with pain.

"You're looking better. Much better than you deserve, but don't worry. I'll fix that soon enough."

"Too bad I can't say the same for you, Sou. You need a wash."

Sou grabbed a wood baton from the side table.

A female guard Ty hadn't noticed cleared her throat and stepped in front of Ty. *Olivia!* She wore the chancellor's security insignia.

"Remember, the chancellor wishes this one to be in perfect health for the meeting. Which I'm here to take him to now." She released his wrists from the cot and bound them together in front before pulling him up to his feet.

"Have a good time, Ty. It's the last good time you're ever going to have."

Ty didn't respond. Surely, Olivia was here to get him out, but how? He tested his psi to find the bands were the same as before. His psi useless.

Olivia winked at him before stepping aside and addressing Sou. "You'll have him back soon enough."

"That's right." Sou slapped the baton in the palm of his hand, repeatedly. "Can't wait." Sou stepped aside as Olivia took Ty's arm and led him from the room.

She pressed a finger to her lips, indicating silence. They stepped into an elevator and the number thirty-two illuminated before the doors closed and they ascended. Releasing his arm, she took out a small silver device. Sliding a switch, all sound faded. "We can talk now."

"What took you so long, beautiful?" Ty asked.

"Oh, you know. The usual. Running for my life. Planning escapes." Her expression turned serious. "They had you so deep, we didn't know where you were. Not until the request to see you came in. It's the woman who took you down, Ty. The one you slept with."

He ignored her disgust-ridden comment and remembered his dream. Running, the rain, and helping Ria. It made no sense. Hallucination? No. Somehow, they'd connected in that dream, or whatever it was. "What's the plan?"

"Stay by the windows. Merek has only one shot to get you out."

Chapter 8

Ria flexed and fisted her hands as Lieutenant Sou escorted her to the interrogation room. He managed to touch her at every turn, which creeped her out and pissed her off in equal measure. Dani had wanted to come along, but since she hadn't officially arrived at the spaceport, they had no way to explain her presence. In hindsight, they should have added the names of all the EPs to Rucon's ship's roster just in case. Rucon would pick her up as soon as she was done here. The hall was wide with offices and interrogation rooms on either side. A standard configuration for any police station. Benches dotted the walls. People sat waiting, either for their turn or for someone, somewhere to finish. A strong odor of antiseptic spoke of frequent cleanings.

Ria's stomach twisted in a knot, and she felt surreal, as though she were in a dream. Their dream.

That's appropriate. She wondered for the millionth time what the frack she was doing here.

Sou stopped at a door near the end of the corridor.

"Wait." She paused.

Ian's voice echoed in her head. *What do you expect is going to happen, even if we can get you in to see him?* He'd asked the question no one else would. She hadn't had an answer for him then, and she didn't have one now.

"Everything all right?" the lieutenant asked. He dripped insincerity as he placed a clammy hand on her arm.

She looked at the door. *No, everything is not all right.* She resisted the urge to slap his hand away. "Everything's fine. Open the door."

Her breath caught at the sight of him. He stood in front of a floor-to-ceiling window with his back to her. Images flashed through her mind:

wet forest, rain falling down the fissure in the mountainside. Their bodies entwined. She expected to be hit with his psi. The pleasure she remembered so well, but there was nothing.

"I'm gonna be right outside this door." Sou said. "You have five minutes." Ty didn't move.

Ria wiped damp palms on her jeans. The door clicked shut behind her. Ty spoke before turning. "Have any interesting dreams lately, Red?"

His voice stunned her. She felt it deep within, confirming her worst fears.

He faced her then, his hands bound in front. Dark hair fell over those gray eyes.

"Don't call me Red." She stepped farther into the room and stopped a few feet away from him. Her next breath brought in his musky scent, which seemed to permeate every cell in her body. *Oh, Goddess, why this man?*

He raised an eyebrow. "Why not call you Red? It suits you."

"I don't like it." That wasn't entirely true. She had liked it the first time. "I'm just here to find out why you killed an unarmed man. And to find out what these dreams mean." She lied about that, too. She knew the second she had entered the room what the dreams meant. He was the one. Her psi-mate. A cold-blooded killer.

"Keep talking, Red." He took a step closer. "I like the sound of your voice. I like the way it feels."

Ria started to speak, but found she had nothing to say. His proximity fired up her psi, but she still couldn't sense his at all. Then she noticed the bands on his wrists.

He shot a glance at the window. "I need to thank you for this visit."

"Yeah? Why?"

With blinding speed, he closed the gap between them, threw his bound hands over her head, and crushed her to his chest. Her brain shorted out. He *smelled* so fucking good. She saw the window over his shoulder explode outward, and they were yanked through the gaping hole. They flew through the air in the grip of a powerful psi. She struggled wildly and looked back to see the door to the room opening and men rushing in, including Sou with a look of astonishment on his face.

Her mind was a jumbled mess. She couldn't make sense of anything with Ty's body pressed against hers. Sensation overload. Her military training kicked in, and she relaxed her muscles, twisted around, and used her hands to fling his arms over her head just as they crashed to the floor of a waiting cruiser. The door sealed shut, and they sped away.

She'd landed half on her side and half on her ass. She held her arms up in front of her, focusing her psi on keeping Ty pinned down. His psi may not be able to leave his body with those bands on, but she was fully enmeshed with it now.

He lurched forward.

"Oh no, you don't." She shoved him against the far side of the cruiser, smacking his head against the glass.

Her body shook. She had to keep him pinned but the very act of connecting with him made her burn with desire.

"Oy, what the frack is this?" A gruff voice bellowed before something smashed into the back of her head, and the lights went out.

* * * *

Ty slid to the floor as soon as Ria lost consciousness. His body and psi still rang with the effect of touching her.

"I thought this was a rescue mission for one," Merek said.

Rolling to his side, Ty shimmied up to the seat next to Merek. "Good to see you, too. You mind?" He held out his bound wrists.

Merek used a laser-knife to sever the cords.

Ty's psi burst out in all directions. Nasty things, psi-bands.

Merek recoiled. "What was that? You all right?"

Ty reached down and picked up the bands. "Mortog has a new toy. These things somehow constrict your psi to your body."

"Isn't that something? Warder Zar just showed these to us."

"Olivia's dad?"

Olivia's father was the head of the Starfall Underground.

"Yep." Merek took the band from Ty gently, as if it was poisonous, and inspected the severed ends. "Bella even tried some on. The Starfall Underground is deeply entrenched in Mortog's government. It gives me hope."

"Yeah." Ty rubbed his chafed skin as he studied the woman at their feet. His action had been total instinct. No thought whatsoever.

Merek reached down and checked her pulse. "She's breathing. I've never seen anyone take you down like that, let alone a waif like this."

The overwhelming buzz she had caused him was fading, but her mere presence provided a continuous feed of some serious energy. He rubbed his back and stretched. "Let's just say she had me at a disadvantage."

"You know who she is, right?"

"Yeah, I know." The anger caused by the thought felt good. Gave him some control over the effect she had on him. "We need to search her."

Merek nodded, and they made short work of locating her com and throwing it out the vehicle.

"Why is she here?" Merek wasn't happy.

Ty shook his head and glanced sideways at his foster father. "Wasn't planned." He looked back at the woman.

"Olivia isn't going to like this." Merek bent over and bound the woman's hands. "This was supposed to be a jail break, not a kidnapping of an off-worlder."

Merek wasn't kidding about Olivia. If Ria really was his psi-mate… *Sandarian fracking military.*

"Seriously, Ty, why'd you bring her?"

"I don't know, okay? Just leave it alone." Her presence here rattled him. His desire for her made him want to punch someone. "Sorry, Merek. They beat me up pretty bad. Had the healers working on me all night. Maybe it messed with my head." *Maybe that's it. It's all in my head.*

As though confirming his suspicion of a head injury, Ty only now thought about the others. "Where's Trin? And Bella? They okay?"

"We're all okay. We've had to go into hiding. The chancellor didn't waste any time. He's got another henchman. They tore our place apart, but we were already gone." The pain in his voice was clear.

"I'm sorry, Merek."

"That wasn't your fault." Merek eyed Ria's still body. "So now you're a murderer and a kidnapper. Frack."

Merek's words stung. He'd killed the father of two innocent children. No one knew better than he what that meant. "Like I said, it wasn't planned. I can't believe I did this any more than you can." Ty thought back to the Ball. To Jara. "I want you to know something."

Merek looked at him with concern. "What is it, son?"

"I wasn't going to go through with it. When I found him, he was talking about kids. His kids." Ty closed his eyes at the memory. "I couldn't do to them what he did to me. I was done. I turned to leave, but he'd seen me. Had my arm and said he knew who I was. He said he was going to take pleasure in killing you and Trin…" Ty swallowed hard at the memory. "He said he was going to keep Bella for himself."

Merek paled. He reached out and put a hand on Ty's shoulder. "Sounds like maybe you saved our lives."

Ty nodded. "We need to figure out how they're finding us. It's got to be someone in Watersedge."

"We think so, too. Arlo's working on it."

Ty looked around. The cruiser skimmed the edge of town. "Why aren't they coming after us?"

"We're cloaked and the cruiser is tagless, no ID. The Starfall Underground has been busy."

"Where are we going?"

"Headquarters. You're not going to believe it. Olivia told us it was big, but she didn't do it justice. We're taking the long way, just in case."

A while later, the interior of the cruiser illuminated as they plunged into an ancient underground transportation tunnel. The cruiser came to a stop not far from the entrance.

"We wait here now for twenty minutes," Merek said, leaning back and lacing his hands behind his head. "You look good."

Ty let out an angry laugh. "Their healers are quite talented."

Merek's jaw clenched. "I'm sorry. Even Warder Zar's people couldn't figure out where you were being kept. They now think it wasn't the jail at all, but the PRs palace."

Ty thought back to the cold room they'd beat him in. "Hard for me to say. I didn't see much, could be though." He ran a hand through his hair. "A private torture chamber. That's quite a palace." He looked around the dark space. "This is interesting."

"This is nothing. Wait till you see their base."

The cruiser started up again twenty minutes later and they continued farther into the tunnels. The vehicle's spotlights illuminated their way as they went deeper into the old network. Finally, they came to a halt at the collapsed end of a tunnel, and the cruiser's door slid open.

"Keep an eye on her," Merek said, stepping out.

Ty looked around the empty tunnel. Nothing approached from the direction they'd come. Merek walked over to the rubble at the end. The debris shimmered and a tall, olive-skinned woman wearing a white T-shirt and cargo pants emerged. Ty smiled and stepped out of the cruiser.

Olivia walked over and planted a kiss on him. "Welcome back."

"Thanks." He brushed a strand of hair from her face. The kiss had been nice. And empty. "So this is the infamous underground, huh?"

"Not quite yet."

Merek cleared his throat, and Ty let Olivia go.

"We have a little problem," Merek said.

"Oh?" Olivia hooked her thumbs on her pockets.

Merek shot Ty a look that seemed to say, "You created this mess."

"Right." Ty stepped aside and motioned to the vehicle.

Olivia looked inside. "Oh, frack. What have you done?"

Ty crossed his arms. "It was a split second decision." Not quite true, but close enough. "She might come in handy."

Olivia scowled at him and spoke into her com. "I need a hood." She turned back to Ty. "Is that who I think it is?"

"Yes."

"Damn it, Ty." Anger and confusion flashed across her face. She crossed her arms and waited in silence.

A moment later, another form approached from the rubble. Olivia indicated the car, and the man climbed in and placed a hood over Ria's head. She let out a groan when the man set her head back down.

"She's waking up," Olivia said. She turned to the man in the cruiser with Ria. "Don't let her see anything and bring the cruiser in. Come on," she said to Ty and Merek. "Time for you to disappear."

Olivia led the way to the debris at the far end. It was a cloaked entrance, the shimmer of the illusion only discernable from close up. Once they passed through, they were back in a dimly lit tunnel. Lights along the ancient walls turned on as they approached and blinked off after they passed.

Olivia kept her distance from Ty and wouldn't look at him. "These lights won't work for anyone not registered with our security." Olivia walked with a quick, sure stride. "We can ride in the cruiser if you want, but I figured you might like to stretch your legs after your recent...accommodations."

"Walking is good," Ty said, matching her stride. "This is impressive."

Olivia made a dismissive sound. "My father started this project over twenty years ago. Wait till you see the hub."

They walked for ten more minutes before they came to another cloaked entrance. Olivia used her psi and half the wall vanished.

Ty stood and took it all in. The "hub" was a massive, cavernous space, three stories tall. It was an old, subterranean station that the underground had brought back to life. Enormous lights illuminated the place like a sunny day on the surface. A few cruisers came and went from tunnels on the perimeter. Large windows showed people going about their business inside. The second floor appeared to be offices while the third looked more like living quarters.

Across the cavern, a group of children ran screaming and laughing in a small playground. The air was surprisingly fresh and, although it was warm, it wasn't hot. It explained Olivia's short sleeves.

Olivia led them inside. "*This* is impressive."

Merek stood at his other side. "Arlo contacted Olivia's father when he heard about your arrest. She arranged to have us brought here until we could get you out of jail."

The reality of the situation hit Ty like a punch in the gut. There was no going home. If Jara hadn't stopped him and said what he did, there was a good chance Merek, Trin, Bella, and he would all be dead. Maybe not Bella. Not yet.

"Are you okay?" Olivia asked almost grudgingly.

He took her hand and kissed it. "I'm sorry about Ria, but she might be useful."

She squeezed his hand and withdrew her own. "We'll see."

"Mortog needs to be stopped," Ty said, changing the subject.

"I'm glad you feel that way." Olivia motioned to the cruiser hovering behind them. "What's your plan for her?"

What was his plan? Ty had no idea. "You have some place to keep her detained?"

"Of course." Olivia gave orders to park the cruiser and take Ria to a holding cell. "Come on. My father wants to meet you, and Trin and Bella are anxious to see you."

Ty and Merek followed along.

A woman entered the playground and rounded up all the kids. Once she got them corralled, she led them inside a nearby door.

"Why are there children here?" Ty asked.

"There's a segment of our population that either choose to live down here, or are, for various reasons, too well known to be integrated into Mitan society. It's not bad here. The education is excellent, and we have a network of houses in or near remote areas all around the planet so no one is permanently underground."

"Unbelievable. You told me it was amazing. You weren't kidding." Ty found the magnitude of their operation hard to absorb.

Merek gave him a nudge. "Kind of makes our Watersedge operation look like a joke, huh?"

Olivia stopped short. "No." She placed a hand on Merek's arm. "Please don't think like that. Watersedge is a welcome part of our family. We are all Curzans. We stick together." She gave Ty a pointed look before leading them into a side entrance and up two flights of stairs to a good-sized room overlooking the open hub below. The moment he entered, Bella bounced out of her chair and wrapped herself around him.

He hugged her back and kissed the top of her head.

Trin came over and hugged him as well, planting a firm kiss on his cheek.

Bella looked up at him, eyes bright. "We didn't know if you'd make it."

"They can't stop me that easily," Ty said. The room held a large oval table surrounded by wheeled chairs. Plush carpet and cream-colored walls made the space inviting.

"Can you believe this place?" Bella gave another squeeze, then ran over to the window.

"Not really, no." Ty turned to the men standing near the head of the table.

They were deep in conversation. The larger, darker-skinned one in the middle must be Olivia's father, Warder Zar. He was an imposing man. His skin a few shades darker than his daughter, he stood a head taller than her and didn't lack for muscle or personality.

"Dad," Olivia said, "this is Ty. Ty, my father, Warder."

Warder shook hands. "About time we met. Sit, please." He finished up with the two men, who then left, eyeing Ty with curiosity.

Olivia didn't miss the looks. "You're kind of a celebrity here."

He sat next to her. Killing Leon may have been the right thing to do, but he couldn't shake the thought of two fatherless children.

Warder took his seat. "Welcome to our little underground."

Everyone sat except Bella, who remained glued to the windows, her fascination with the place obvious. An older woman and a teen came in pushing a cart. The smell of something delicious had Ty's mouth watering. They placed trays of food in the center of the table and passed out plates and bottled drinks.

"Don't suppose they fed you much in that hellhole," Warder said. "Help yourself. Same for the rest of you. Thanks, Marta."

The old woman shooed the teen out and patted Warder on the shoulder. "You just call when you want it cleared."

"Will do."

Ty grabbed a large sandwich and water. The juicy meat melted in his mouth. After a week of nothing but sustenance packets, the sandwich was perfection.

"Now," Warder said, "down to business. First, you appear in good shape, ya?"

Ty nodded, his mouth full.

"Good, well done Merek," Warder said.

"Couldn't have done any of it without your help."

"You're welcome." Warder took a drink of a dark liquid. "I have spent considerable time speaking with Father Arlo. The Watersedge operation may be small, but up until five or six months ago, it was airtight. I think you are all correct in believing there is a mole."

Merek and Trin nodded agreement.

"Is Arlo here?" Ty asked.

"No," Warder said. "All indications are he's safe at the moment. We have people inside Mortog's security office. They aren't yet placed to be able to tell us everything, but the intel is getting better all the time. Once we get the four of you settled, Olivia will go to work with Arlo on forming surveillance teams from your own people. If the security force shows up in Watersedge, the team will know what to do. We can't risk putting all your people in hiding for two reasons. First, there are simply too many to absorb and second, until we catch your mole, it would be an unacceptable security risk. It's going to be cat-and-mouse until Mortog is removed from power. Not elegant, but it's the best we can do for now."

Trin leaned in. "You have our eternal gratitude."

"We are Curzan. United we will take back what is rightfully ours."

"We should take it back now," Olivia said. "We know Mortog's schedule."

"That is nothing but a battle," Warder said with some exasperation. "We need to win the war."

It was clear this wasn't a new conversation. Olivia shoved her hands into her pockets. Ty knew how she felt, but understood the wisdom of her father's words. He himself had won a battle, and yet the war remained.

"Now, about these books." Warder leaned back in his chair and crossed his arms.

"You know about the texts?" Ty asked. Arlo hadn't shared that with anyone but Merek's household.

"Yes. In fact, I told Arlo that Olivia might be able to assist. She takes to languages easily."

Olivia relaxed some. "I've taught myself three languages so far. I'd love to see what you have."

"Sure," Ty said. The thought of working with her wasn't a bad one.

"We could use a fresh set of eyes," Bella said, coming over for some food.

"Then we agree," Warder said. "A runner is out now to get the books. Arlo and I felt they would be safer with you in hiding."

"Good," Bella said. "I can show you when they arrive."

"You can show me when we get you settled. The hub is currently full, but we have a place in mind." Olivia smiled at the teen. "First, we have a minor, or should I say small, complication to deal with."

Ty had nearly forgotten about Ria. "She comes with us."

"Ty—"

"Not open to discussion. I'd like a cruiser for the two of us on the way out there."

The hurt in Olivia's eyes stabbed him with guilt.

"Something we should know?" Warder asked, looking from Ty to Olivia.

"I just need to talk to her. Alone."

Warder considered a minute. "All right. But you'll not be having control of the vehicle. It will follow the others."

"That's fine," Ty said, wondering what the frack he was doing.

"Are you sure about this?" Merek asked under his breath.

Ty just nodded.

Olivia cussed under her breath but called someone and told them to bring Ria out in fifteen minutes for departure.

Everyone ate their fill before they headed downstairs to the cruisers. Two men led Ria over to the cruiser they were taking. She still wore the hood, so they helped her into the vehicle. Once inside, they locked her into restraints. Ty noticed they'd added a set of psi-bands on her wrists. He almost felt sorry for her.

Olivia approached with a backpack slung over one shoulder. "It's all over the vids now. Your escape and the kidnapping of an off-worlder security agent. From the looks of her, she won't be much trouble."

Given the way she'd pinned him in the cruiser, Ty wasn't so sure. And then there was the effect she had on him. "Where are we going?"

"I talked it over with my father. We don't want to keep you here. It's too close to Starfall. If she managed to escape, she might be able to get to the surface. And given there are now five of you, plus me, off and on to help with the texts, we need a good-sized place. We have an eight-bedroom hunting lodge deep in the Trillion Forest. She escapes from there, and she won't make it out alive."

"Sounds cozy," Bella said, holding her own backpack and looking a little freaked.

Olivia turned to the teen. "You'll be fine as long as you stay inside the perimeter of the repeller field."

* * * *

Loc Zorton's office overlooked the city of Ardos. As the capital of Sandaria, it was, by design, the most visually stunning city on the planet. A summer storm raged outside. Dangerous and beautiful, it produced an erratic dance of purple and green clouds that swirled high in the atmosphere. When the mass and velocity of the gasses reached certain limits, explosions shook the lower atmosphere. The violence matched his own emotions.

A knock at the door pulled his attention back. "Come."

Old Merrin ambled in and bowed slightly, but not enough to show the respect owed to the leader of the guild. As always, his robes were wrinkled and hung askew on his shoulders.

"What news?"

Merrin instructed his aide to wait outside. Once the door closed, he ambled over to Loc's desk and situated himself into one of the three guest chairs. He took his time.

Loc's anger rose as he waited for the man to settle.

"It has begun."

"I assume you are referring to the abduction of Vertan citizens."

Merrin nodded.

"How many?"

"Only two so far. They are on the trail of a third that escaped."

Loc turned back to the storm. He silently cursed the eleven Portal Masters who had escaped to Earth. If he ever got them back…of course, they would live. The guild needed their psi, but their lives would be misery. He would see to it.

Never in the history of the guild had their secrets been so close to being exposed. Finding Sandarians with strong enough psi to become Portal Masters, and convincing them to do so, was a slow and tedious process. Not many men were willing to give up their future families and lives for the guild. Once they joined, they were Portal Masters for life and would remain in the compound. It had been a hard truth to swallow. Loc himself had believed the guild was a religious order that served a god. A god that spoke only to a select few. The elders had explained to him, upon his election as head of the guild, the religion was a ruse. Another means to keep those indoctrinated in the compound. It was not a terrible fate. The walled grounds spanned nearly a mile. Once they had resided outside the town of Ardos, but after five hundred years, Ardos and its suburbs surrounded the compound. Because of their source of power, the mysterious orb deep underground, they could never move. Or so he'd been told. To this day, the origins of the object were still a mystery.

And now, they were severely restricted in the number of masters needed to create portals. Requests had been coming in from the new GTO. Requests they had not fulfilled. With the Portal Masters remaining on Sandaria, there was only a limited number of portals they could create. They needed to get enough Vertans to implement their plan. They would create portals with the alternate psi. They would retain their control. He would see to it.

Loc turned back to Merrin. "We need more than three Vertans."

"Indeed. Our previous efforts to contain the citizens to their planet were highly effective. In order to fulfill our quota, the Torogs ask permission to abduct the required number directly from Vertan itself."

Loc grimaced. It was dirty business, ripping people from their lives. "You have my permission. Where are the two you have now?"

"On their way from Florin 5."

"And the new compound?"

"It will be complete within the week, before their arrival."

They'd agreed that the captive Vertans would live in a separate compound far from the city of Ardos. They would remain there for the rest of their lives, serving the guild.

Loc soothed his conscience with the knowledge that the guild would treat them exceptionally well, as long as they behaved. There were worse fates that could befall a soul. "Fine. Keep me up to date."

Instead of standing to go, Merrin remained seated.

"Is there more?"

"We have a problem."

"Ha. Other than trying to contain an entire planet? Or implementing a plan that requires us to acquire and imprison over a dozen hostages? Do tell, Master Merrin."

Merrin steepled his fingers and gazed at Loc over their tips. "Portals are failing."

"That's not funny, old man."

"Then I suggest you pay attention. We neglected to tell you everything about the guild."

Anger washed over him, and Loc wondered how many more secrets they'd kept from him. "Surely, it cannot be worse than our current issues."

"Much worse."

Loc ground his teeth in an effort to remain calm. "Explain how it is that portals can fail."

"One of the reasons we go out of our way to ensure no one leaves the compound has to do with how the portals are sustained. Once a master helps create a portal, he is tied to it forever."

"And?"

"And a large number of our masters are absent. The Portals can sustain themselves for only so long. Under normal conditions, they pull from the master's psi as needed. That cannot happen if the Portal Masters are not present. They fail."

Loc leaned back in his chair, stunned. Shock turned to rage, and he slammed his fist down on his desk. "I am the head of the guild. There are to be no more secrets. Would you care to tell me on whose authority this information was withheld from me?"

Merrin rose slowly to his feet. "I think we both know the answer to that. You may be head of the guild but do not think for one moment that you have all the power."

Rage burned inside of Loc. "Well then, I suggest you get your little Torogs moving. If you fail to pull off this plan, I will hold you responsible under guild law."

"Fool." Merrin snarled. "If this plan fails, there will be no guild."

Chapter 9

That son of a crag's mate is going to pay for this. Someone had given Ria a bottle of water, but other than that, she'd been bound hand and foot *like a fracking criminal* and kept hooded. It didn't take long to discover whatever they had tied her up with somehow bound her psi to her body. As much as she hated ties, she appreciated their usefulness.

After an hour or so, they packed her back into a vehicle, restraining her body to the seat. She wasn't going anywhere, but she'd be safe in a crash—how comforting. A short time later, voices spoke outside the cruiser, but she couldn't make out what was being said. Ty was there. She knew that. She *felt* that. The door opened on the other side of the vehicle.

Ty. She recognized his psi, his energy. There was an underlying musk to the way he smelled, so much like her favorite perfume. *Time for a new scent.*

From the sound of it, he was in the back compartment. Probably facing her. A slight motion told her they were moving.

"Enjoying yourself, Red?"

His voice resonated deep within. She tried to lean back, get some distance, but there was no place to go. "I told you not to call me that."

"And I told you it suits you. Even if your hair is mostly covered at the moment."

"Yeah, about that. Get this thing off me."

"Can't do that until we get where we're going." Anger edged his voice.

"Why did you bring me with you?"

"None of your business."

"Are you insane?"

* * * *

Was he? Maybe. From the moment Ty had slipped into the car, he knew proximity was going to be a problem with her. He sensed her presence like magnetic north and knew she'd feel it, too. That's why he'd asked to take the ride out to the lodge with her alone. He'd keep his distance moving forward but needed to set some rules. At least that's what he told himself. And who knew? Maybe he was insane. Twenty minutes later, they were deep into the forest, flying low over the treetops. He leaned forward, elbows on knees, and studied her. She smelled of fresh soap and something else. "We won't hurt you if you cooperate. Where we're going there is no escape, so don't even think about it."

"You haven't answered my question." The hood muffled her voice.

Ty ran his hands through his hair. Riding with her, this close for so long, wasn't such a good idea. His desire grew with every second. The cabin smelled of...them.

With lightening speed, he reached over and pulled the hood off her head.

Her head jerked up, eyes wide. He stared into their green depths.

Her breath hitched as their psi connected. "You didn't tell me you were Curzan."

Pleasure coursed through him at the sound of her voice. "You didn't ask." He partially stood and placed his hands on the seat on either side of her. He leaned closer and inhaled deeply. Inches from her ear, he said, "Maybe I am insane." He brushed his lips against her neck. Memories flooded back of their night together. The touch of her skin ignited his psi as pleasure coursed through him.

Her body shivered, but she didn't resist. No, she leaned her head back, giving him better access. He trailed his tongue along her collarbone and back up to her jaw. She tasted salty sweet and her smell was intoxicating.

Energy built up inside as he inhaled her aroma, then exhaled a long, low growl. She moaned in response and turned to meet his lips with her own. Their psi erupted in waves of pleasure as their tongues danced around each other. Goddess help him, but he wanted to consume this woman. It was a foreign sensation with the psi-bands on. Only by touching her could he feel her psi. Her skin. She was soft and silky and he needed more. *She was Sandarian military.*

Ty flung himself backward and slid as far away from her as possible. He'd done it again. Just like at the jail. No thought had occurred before he was next to her, running his lips down that silky neck.

Sandarian military.

His heart pounded, and he clenched his fists, letting the anger build. "Rule number one, we stay away from each other."

"Ya think?" Her eyes flashed with anger of her own as she wiped her lips with bound hands.

"Rule number two, the bands stay on at all times. No psi. You're outnumbered and out-gunned."

Her eyes narrowed, but she said nothing.

"I don't want this to be any harder than necessary. Where we're going doesn't lend itself to escape. You try, you die. You behave, and you'll have more freedoms. You got that?"

She remained silent, which was probably just as well. The more she spoke, the more his psi resonated with her energy. A twinge of the pleasure he'd felt when he kissed her trickled down his spine. *She's military. Sandarian fracking military. I should dump her in the forest and let the woricks take care of her.*

* * * *

Ria sat rigid, looking into liquid gray eyes. Eyes, no doubt, that belonged to her psi-mate. Darl said Curzans were thought to be little better than animals. What Ty did to her body and psi made her sick at heart. Her system was in shock. With nothing more than a touch from him, her brain short-circuited. All thoughts ceased as pleasure took over. Her lack of control terrified her. The fact that he'd pulled away pissed her off because she knew, even if she'd been able, she wouldn't have.

Aside from that one snarky response, she couldn't talk. Wouldn't talk. She had no idea what words would come out of her mouth if she did.

They spent the rest of the ride in silence. More and more, Ria wanted out of the cruiser. Like an attack of claustrophobia, she fought a feeling of panic. The cords around her wrists didn't help any. His closeness undermined her resolve. She couldn't help but remember his touch. Finally, the cruiser slowed and descended, and she welcomed the distraction. Through the canopy of trees below, she could make out a large dwelling of some kind. It was well camouflaged and easily missed if you didn't know what to look for. The cruiser pulled into a large barn next to two other vehicles.

Ty was out the door before the vehicle touched down. As soon as he left, her anxiety subsided, and she breathed easier.

The vehicles were parked in one corner of the barn. She recognized the massive animals in stalls along one wall. Like horses on Earth, only stockier with shorter necks and longer legs, thick as tree trunks. Strong and sturdy, nothing spooked them, which made them excellent mounts for hunting. Ty told her she couldn't escape. *You try, you die.* His voice echoed with a shiver down her spine.

Ria counted five people as they left the barn and headed for the main building. There was a massive bulk of a man holding the arm of a shorter, stout woman. A teenage girl and an exotic looking beauty were talking to Ty.

Good. She can keep him out of my hair. Two other men unloaded crates onto a hovering platform and followed the others. Pet goons, how nice. She tested her restraints and wasn't surprised when they didn't budge. Scanning the large space, she made mental note of everything stored along the walls. It was sparse, but there were a few things that might help during an escape.

You better watch your back, Ty Sordina, because you picked the wrong person to mess with. Even the thought of his name riled her insides.

They left her there for a good fifteen minutes before one of the goons came out and released her seat restraints. She stepped out of the cruiser and stretched as best she could before letting him lead her out of the barn.

The thick smell of the forest was everywhere. The woods were dense, and off in the distance, came the faint sound of water. Above the treetops, mountain peaks soared, blocking the direct light of Mitah's sun. They climbed a flight of steps to the front entrance and went inside. A massive great room with an oversized fireplace greeted them. Heads of animals, some with hair, others with thick looking hides, adorned the walls. Large, small, reptilian, it was all there. Numerous paintings depicting scenes of hunts covered the remaining space.

Ria wasn't sure what to expect. The goons were clearly security dudes, but the others didn't seem to be. Ty's family maybe? Except for the woman. She was beautiful and carried herself with confidence. Unless Ria was wrong, she also had the hots for Ty. She desperately wanted not to care about that. Really, really wanted not to care. She tried to ignore the sensation spreading through her as she remembered his touch.

Goon dudes didn't seem to know what to do with her so they all just stood in the entryway.

Footsteps echoed closer from the other end of the room. The large man she'd seen earlier emerged from a hallway on the far side. He paused a moment when he saw her, then came forward with a determined look on his face. He stopped a pace in front of her. Head tilted slightly, he reached out a hand. "Name's Merek."

* * * *

Stewing, Mortog paced in his office. The jailbreak of Ty Sordina was unthinkable. The imbecile had taken the EP as well, or had she been part of the escape? He drummed his fingers on his polished wood desk. Having heard the news, Rucon Cavacent was on his way over. Normally, this wouldn't present a problem, but it appeared the man was impervious to Mortog's special skill. That made him dangerous. He'd have ordered him killed if not for his connections within the military. Still, perhaps there was a way.

His com buzzed. "What is it?"

"You have a call, your excellency," his secretary said. "It is from the newly appointed president of Sandaria, Gordat Prayda."

Mortog pondered the call. The Cavacents had fled Sandaria for a reason. In his previous role as a councilman, Prayda was well known for having similar views to his own. Perhaps this day was taking a turn for the better. "Put him through." He waited a beat. "This is Chancellor Mortog. What can I do for you Mr. President?"

"I understand a Cavacent EP recently apprehended a criminal on your planet."

So, Mortog thought, he knows about the capture of the boy, but not their escape. "That is correct. The clan was here for the Summer's Ball."

"Ah, then I suppose they are no longer guests of your planet?"

Mortog could tell Prayda was fishing, but for what? "Actually, there has been an unfortunate turn of events. EP Montori was due to leave for Earth today, but she appears to have been kidnapped by the killer during his escape. That, or she is responsible for his escape."

"Really?" The president sounded quite happy about that. "Are the rest of them on Mitah?"

"Only Rucon. I believe the rest are on their way. Might I ask why this interests you?"

"The Portal Masters have requested that I assist them in retrieving some things that were stolen from them. As well as nearly a dozen masters, one of Rucon's EPs is a tall albino by the name of Armond. He took a small black device from the guild, and they would like it, and the albino, back. As for myself, I'm not a fan of Rucon. If you could perhaps detain him…"

Having the Portal Masters as an ally would be of immeasurable benefit. They operated outside the law in their own world. "I would be happy to assist the guild and you in any way possible. I'm assuming, of course, they would be willing to return the favor."

"Indeed, they would be very grateful. I have already dispatched three Portal Masters to Mitah. When they arrive, we will establish the gateway, and we will discuss this in person."

The day was indeed looking up. "It would be my pleasure."

* * * *

Rucon entered Chancellor Mortog's office enraged. This planet had been nothing but trouble from the start. Mortog was on his com chewing out the weasel Sou and demanding he return at once. He disconnected and faced Rucon. He stood without a word for a long pause. "You arranged for her to meet him alone. I find that suspiciously convenient."

Idiot. "My team apprehended him in the first place. Why would we break him out now?"

Mortog leaned over and slammed his fist onto his desk. "I don't know. Perhaps you planned to rescue him all along and my security got in your way?"

Rucon stepped up to the desk, placed his palms on the surface, and stared the man down, ignoring the twinge at the back of his neck. "We had to wait for your security to show up and take him into custody. There are only two families that I or any of my clan know on this planet of yours. One of those families has recently suffered a tragic loss. Do you really think I would rescue his killer? Face it Mortog, this is homegrown. My clan has nothing to do with it. Now, this is your planet and I want my EP back. Am I clear?"

The chancellor flushed an unflattering shade of red. "You'll get your EP when I get my killer."

Rucon stood straight, knowing he couldn't force the man's hand. He'd already told him the EPs were returning, but what he didn't know is that they were already here. They'd find the killer all right. The twinge in the back of his head increased, and he finally realized what it was. It was a rare psi talent that he'd only experienced once. "Are you attempting to direct my thoughts?"

The feeling stopped abruptly.

"Pity you weren't more susceptible, but then it will be much more fun for me this way." Mortog flipped a hand, and five armed guards entered the room.

"You can't be serious," Rucon said.

"I assure you I can." He addressed the guards. "Disarm him, put him in psi-bands and lock him up. He's got a visitor coming."

"You won't get away with this."

"I already have. Take him away."

By the time Lieutenant Sou showed up, Mortog's mood was much improved. The possibility of being able to requisition a portal without the usual costs and delays pleased him greatly. "Any word on how they managed to escape?"

"No, sir. They used a tagless vehicle and seem to have simply vanished."

"No one simply vanishes. They obviously had help. Jara was convinced there was a coordinated effort among the Curzans. It is time we increase our search." Mortog strode to the windows and took in the gardens beyond. "The so-called underground of Curzan vile must be put to an end." He swung around.

Sou backed up a few steps.

"Find them. They are about to murder a very prominent citizen of the GTO and a good friend of Supreme Commander Anantha. And because of this heinous act, they must be punished. It's all coming together very nicely, don't you think?"

Confusion played across Sou's face. "Sir?"

"Lord Rucon Cavacent is going to be murdered by the Curzans."

Sou smiled. "That's brilliant."

"Find the boy that Jara was using as a source and bring him to me."

Chapter 10

Merek led Ria to a good-sized room on the second floor of the lodge. There was a large bed, a small sitting area, and a desk. A door stood off to the side, which she figured was either a closet or a bathroom. Bars covered the two windows that looked out over the back of the property. The floor was carpeted and the window draped with curtains. It was better than a jail cell.

Merek motioned toward the desk. "You'll be needing some things. There's stuff to write with over there. Make a list with your clothes sizes, and we'll see what we can do." He seemed to wait for a reply.

She tried to cross her arms, was thwarted by the psi-bands, so just stood there. The fact they were going to supply her with "things" meant they weren't going to kill her. Not immediately, anyway.

"Suit yourself," Merek said. "I expect you're hungry." He didn't say anything more before turning to go.

She checked the door and wasn't surprised to find it locked. Prowling the perimeter of the room, she looked for anything that might be useful. Frustration at her detainment fought with the hunger in her stomach. As if on cue, she heard the lock click on the door and Merek was back, this time with the teenager in tow with a tray of food.

Merek stepped aside for the girl. "Put it on the table."

The dark-haired girl set the tray down on the coffee table and openly checked out Ria. Her psi lightly brushed against Ria's, and she stepped closer. "You don't look or feel like a Curzan killer."

"Bella," Merek snapped.

The teen smiled. "That's my name, don't wear it out." She winked at Ria before leaving.

Merek locked the door when they left, but Ria could still hear them. "What was that?" he asked the girl.

"I think Ty is wrong about her, that's all."

Their voices faded, and Ria regarded the food. There was a sandwich of some kind, some fruit, and a couple bottles of water. She sat down and took a bite of the sandwich. Thinking about what the girl said to Merek, she wondered. The girl had brushed her psi with enough contact for Ria to read her fairly well. There wasn't any overt malice in her. She had a healthy dose of anger toward Sandarians in general, and Mitans in particular, but she herself seemed decent. And intelligent. Like Ty. And Merek, for that matter. They were nothing like Ria had been led to expect from Curzans. She took another bite and thought of Ty. Their night together had been crazy with passion and a pleasure that was nearly blinding. She hadn't really focused on Ty himself, but she'd picked up enough at dinner to know he wasn't dangerous to her. The attraction had been mutual, and she'd focused on that.

As to who or what he was on a deeper level, it was hard to say. He short-circuited her brain when he was near. She knew virtually nothing about him. She thought about the others. They'd rescued Ty and kidnapped her. Well, he'd kidnapped her. They had contacts somewhere. They must in order to have pulled off not just the jailbreak, but the disappearing act, too. And this lodge was no cabin in the woods. This cost money. Lots of money. These were no animals she was dealing with.

Or maybe I'm just lying to myself because I can't stand the thought of bonding with an immoral sub-human.

Ria ate everything on her plate. She was going to need all the energy she could get because one thing was for certain. She wasn't staying here.

* * * *

The following morning the teen came alone with the food.

"It's Bella, right?" Ria asked.

"So you can talk."

"Yeah." Ria smiled at her. "You seem like a decent enough person from what I could tell with our contact yesterday."

Bella stood and regarded her. "You read people?"

Ria nodded. "You?"

"I guess. You seem like a nice person, too. Not at all what Ty said."

"I can't read him very well," Ria admitted, hoping to gain the girl's confidence. "He probably has the same problem with me."

"Why? I can always read people."

Ria couldn't tell her they were probably psi-mates so she hedged with the one answer even a teen couldn't argue with. "I don't know. It's weird."

Bella nodded, apparently satisfied. She put the tray down on the table. She glanced briefly at Ria's bound wrists but didn't offer to remove them.

Ria smiled, a plan forming in her head.

* * * *

She'd been there for three days and was beyond bored. They hadn't activated the vid screen so there wasn't much she could do. The amount of exercise possible with her wrists bound was limited at best. Her frustration and agitation were increasing with every day. Or more specifically, every night. There was no staying away from Ty when she slept. The first two nights, she'd had the same dream as before. They were running from someone. The fear was real, as was the pain of the laser piercing her side. Last night was different. They hadn't been running. They'd been making love. Her body shook with the memory. Gods, she could even smell him now. She couldn't do this any longer.

She'd made progress with Bella. It wasn't hard since they genuinely liked each other. A pang of guilt surged at the thought of deceiving the teen, but she had no choice. If she stayed here, like this, she'd self combust.

As usual, Bella brought her a tray for dinner that night. She'd hung out a few times, asking questions about space travel and other planets. She was particularly interested in interstellar ships. The logistics of building a space-worthy vehicle and the mystery of interstellar portals fascinated her to no end.

After the usual barrage of questions, Bella stood to go. "Thanks, Ria. I'll let you finish your dinner. I have to go help with the laundry." She pouted at the thought.

"After being stuck in here for the last three days, I'd love to help do laundry."

"I'll talk to Merek," Bella said. "We can't keep you locked in here forever."

"Thanks." Ria figured it was now or never. "Bella, do you think you could remove my bands? Just at night. It's really hard to sleep with my wrists tied."

Ria held her breath while Bella hesitated a long moment.

"I suppose," Bella said, reaching into her pocket. "Don't tell anyone, okay?"

"I won't."

"And don't try to escape. I'm serious. We're in the middle of worick country. Without a repeller, you won't last the night."

Her concern was heartfelt.

"Don't worry," Ria said. "I've seen vids of those things. I wouldn't go near one."

Bella released the band, and Ria's psi burst out.

"Wow, that feels good." Ria stretched her arms wide, wincing as her muscles protested.

Bella smiled and left the band on the coffee table. "I'll see you in the morning, okay?"

"In the morning. Thanks, Bella."

After Bella left, Ria went to work. She'd checked out the bars on the windows the first night here. They were a single unit, the bars attached to a quarter-inch thick metal slab on top and bottom. She'd yanked on both and found the one on the left was coming loose from the window frame. She couldn't budge it without her psi, but was pretty sure it would come off easily now. Waiting was the hardest part. She was bound to make some noise and wanted to make sure most, if not all, the people were asleep. It was a little after two in the morning when she made her move. She'd stayed awake, not wanting to risk a connection with Ty. There was no telling what he might be able to pick up now that the bands were off.

She slid the window open and made short work of the bars. After three days, using her psi was exhilarating. She lowered the assembly to the ground outside and followed after. Her room had nothing she could use as a weapon so she made her way to the barn. Sliding in quietly, she closed the door behind her. Glow lights lined the walls and ceiling, giving off a cozy feel. The barn smelled of the large hunting beasts and animal feed. Rifling through the tack box she found a sharp pick, probably used to clean the animals' hooves. She slid it into her pocket and moved over to a workbench along the side. A sheathed knife with a five-inch blade was the only other useful item she could find. No laser blades, no darts, nothing. She briefly entertained the idea of taking one of the animals, but with the forests filled with woricks, stealth was her best weapon.

She left through a small door out the back of the barn and headed toward the hills. She'd need to get higher to figure out where she was and determine the best direction to go. She was also fairly certain woricks couldn't climb. If she could scale the cliff face and get out of their reach, she had a good chance of making it out. At least, she hoped she did.

Ty's presence had been an underlying buzz at the lodge, sometimes fading, but always present. The farther away she traveled, the weaker the buzz became. The night was cool and both moons were high in the sky. There was plenty of light as long as she stayed out from underneath the trees, but that wasn't always possible as she wanted to take the most direct route.

She was nearly at the base, just a few hundred yards from the cliffs, when her instincts kicked in. Fear prickled her skin, then she heard it. Rustling in the distance. She stopped and listened. There. Her heart rate quickened as she realized there was more than one of whatever was out there. A lot more. They were to her right so she angled left, which took her away from the cliffs, but she had no choice. She picked up her speed. Anytime she came to an obstruction that would require her to make noise, she simply jumped it using her psi. Nothing drained psi energy faster than levitation so she used it sparingly.

She jumped another fallen tree and landed badly. Falling forward, she crashed into thick bushes and cried out as something tore into her arm. A branch had pierced her forearm. The stick was firmly attached to the bush and too green to break. She said a silent prayer it hadn't pierced an artery, gritted her teeth, and pulled her arm off. Her head swam with the pain, and she swallowed the scream threatening to give her away. She waited a beat to make sure no blood came spurting out before taking off again.

An eerie howl echoed through the trees. They'd scented her. The hunt was on. She gave up on stealth and ran for it. Pushing her fear aside, she slipped into combat mode and focused on surviving.

* * * *

Ty tossed and turned in bed. Half awake and half asleep, he drifted. He knew what was coming. Since he'd brought her here, it happened every night. Except last night. That had been different. The passion of the dream burned through him. He tried to push it aside, but it wouldn't go.

She was running. The mountains were close, but something was wrong. The moons shone above, bright against the rocks leading up to the cliff face.

Ty rolled over and punched his pillow a few times before settling back down.

The woricks outside were on the hunt. Their yapping and howling drifted in his open window, hard to ignore. He grabbed a pillow and pulled it over his head.

She ran fast. But not fast enough. They were getting closer.

Moons. Ty bolted upright. In their dream it was always raining. He flew out of bed and ran the length of the hall. Turning the corner, he used his psi and found her door locked. He stopped outside and caught his breath. Maybe he was wrong.

Outside, the woricks' frantic hunting cries echoed through the night.

Oh, frack. He unlocked the door and pushed it open. Her bed lay empty, and the curtains on one of the windows rustled in the breeze. He ran over and looked down. The bars lay on the ground below.

Ty spun around and ran back to his room. He threw on a pair of jeans and shoes and pulled a T-shirt over his head. He unlocked his arms locker and withdrew a dart, grabbed another for good measure, then activated and pocketed three repellers. Normally one would be sufficient, but if they had her cornered or worse, their frenzy could override the pain caused by the small devices.

She stumbled hard, but managed to keep going. The sounds of the pack were close, too close.

Ty shook his head, more and more images of hers superseded his own vision. He smelled the forest. A moment of clarity hit him, and he stopped. This was crazy. He should get help. He moved to call Merek when she cried out.

They were on her.

Ty didn't waste time navigating the lodge, he jumped from his window and took off running. The pull of her psi guided him through the woods, but he would have found her anyway. The frenzied barking and yapping of the woricks bounced off the mountains.

She stood backed against a dense stand of trees. It was a good strategy. The animals had to come at her head on. One of the beasts lunged, and she slashed at its throat. Its lifeless jaws tore at the skin of her forearm. The smell of blood sent the rest of the pack into a craze. She threw the beasts nearest her against the rest of the pack with psi, but she was weakening.

Ty was close. He recognized the stench of the animals ahead. He broke into the small clearing and lunged between Ria and three attacking woricks. Switching to sword mode, he swung the laser in an arc as he whirled and placed himself between them and her. Screams pierced the night as the creatures fell to the ground.

Ty planted his feet, his back to Ria and a laser in each hand.

The animals barked and whined as the repellers overcame their desire to feed. They turned in circles and made a few feeble attempts to lunge, nipping at each other in frustration. Ty didn't blame the beasts. This was their territory, and they had to eat like any other animal. He hollered and swung the laser. Finally, after one last attempt to overcome the repellers, the alpha worick snarled and took off into the woods. The others followed suit, anxious to escape the painful repellers.

Ty spun around. Ria stood there, shaking, blood dripping from her arm. He pulled her to him and let their psi caress. She was near exhaustion but gained strength quickly as he fed her his own energy. She rested her head against his chest until they were balanced. He pulled away and looked into her eyes. "That was a really stupid move."

"I had to get away from you. From us."

In that instant, he knew he could never let that happen. He shook his head. Her right arm was bleeding. There was a puncture wound that went all the way through her forearm and a jagged tear, or maybe bite marks, below that. "You're a mess, Red." *A beautiful fracking mess.*

She stood perfectly still as he placed his fingers on either side of the hole, her blood slick under his fingers. The psi connection necessary to heal flowed through them both. He had to place his other hand against the bark of the tree she leaned against to steady himself. Once the bleeding stopped, he placed his fingers over the tear. Another deep connection to stop the bleeding, and they both moaned.

The pleasure caused by their psi connection was overwhelming. This was no mere chemistry. She was his psi-mate. There was no question now. Once the bleeding stopped, he let go of her arm.

Her eyes bore into him, and he was lost. He took her hand and led her deeper into the forest until he found the trail he was looking for. They followed it in silence. She never once asked where he was taking her. Their psi danced, and the tension between them increased with every step. Finally, they came to the small one-room hunting shack he'd been coming to in order to get some distance from her.

Ironic.

As they neared the porch, the moonlight caught her hair, and it blazed red. He reached out and pulled a leaf from her tresses before leading her inside.

He knew she wouldn't protest. She couldn't stop this anymore than he could. Their psi were deeply meshed together now and simply awaited their bodies to join. They took off their clothes quickly and finally came together with nothing between them.

* * * *

Ria's body erupted in ecstasy as he pulled her close. She wrapped her arms around his neck and kissed him deeply. He lifted her up and she wrapped her legs around his waist. She moaned as she ground herself against his erection. He carried her to the bed, and she held tight as he positioned them in the center of the mattress. Every touch sent a world of sensation through her. She explored every inch of him, frenzied and frantic. Part of her wanted to go slow and savor every second, but she couldn't. Not now. She opened her legs, and he settled between her thighs. He trailed a hand from her neck to her breast. Cupping it, he took the nipple into his mouth. Heat exploded as his tongue teased her. He bit and nibbled his way back up her neck before claiming her lips with his own. He moved his hips, rubbing against her, increasing her need for him.

She cried out with the sensation. "Yes. Oh, Gods, Ty. Please, finish this."

He growled and leaned down to bite her neck. "You're mine now, Ria."

She returned his growl, grabbed hold of his hair, and made him look at her. "And you are mine."

He took her then, plunging deep inside her. A cry escaped her lips. It wasn't possible. Two bodies together couldn't feel this good. He moved faster, and she matched his rhythm. Opposing thrusts as their psi pulsed with each plunge. So close to coming, her psi took over and the world exploded. Her vision turned gray and green. On some level, she sensed her body but stayed focused on their psi.

"It's ours now." Ria was in awe that she could feel his psi like her own. He laughed, and his joy washed over her. Surprising, shocking.

Their psi swirled together, faster, and she thrilled at the sensation. It was as though their psi formed another corporeal body, one they shared. Together they played, dancing on another plane before reality slowly crept in.

Images flashed across Ria's mind. With each came emotions of who he was. Memories and faces drifted by.

He must be experiencing the same from her.

Then, two faces and a stab of loss so real it took her breath.

Their psi unfurled in an instant, and she was back in her body with Ty wrapped around her. She lay curled against him, her head on his chest. He held her tight, his eyes pressed closed. The rapid beat of his heart slowed, comforting her as the reality of what had just happened sunk in. A conflicted barrage of emotion hit her.

He squeezed tighter but still held his eyes shut.

She'd felt terrible pain. Something that had torn him apart. Something she knew nothing about. She remembered the two faces and had no idea who they were. In truth, she had no idea who this man in her arms, *her psi-mate*, really was.

Chapter 11

An incessant buzzing woke Ty. He and Ria had drifted off, and judging by the light outside the windows, it was well past sunrise. He used his psi to retrieve his jeans and pulled his com out of the pocket. Ria looked up at him and took his breath away. She was beautiful, she was his, and she was Sandarian. Rolling from the bed, she grabbed her clothes from the floor before heading for the bathroom. Her body was lean and muscled. Her breasts small and perfect. Ty pulled himself up and leaned against the headboard before connecting with Merek.

"Hey."

"Where are you? Are you all right? Is she with you? Goddess, what do you think you're doing running off in the middle of the night? Did you hear the woricks? Was that you? Frack. Tell me you're okay."

He heard Trin's worried voice in the background rattling off her own questions.

"I'm fine. Ria's fine." Ty glanced at the bathroom door. It didn't seem right to blurt out that he'd just bonded with his psi-mate. They'd figure it out soon enough. "She escaped. I had to go after her."

"Bella took off her psi-bands."

From his tone of voice, Ty figured he was looking at the teen. He had to smile. "It's all right. Sorry I didn't wake you. I was going to but...I heard the woricks and knew she was in trouble. Another thirty seconds, and she would have been gone." The thought ripped through him. It was difficult to reconcile his need for her and his hatred for Sandarians.

Merek blew out a heavy sigh. "Where are you? I'll come and pick you up."

Ty sent their location to Merek's com. "Give us fifteen okay?"

There was a long pause on the other end before Merek said, "All right then. I'll see you in fifteen."

He tossed his com down and waited for Ria to emerge. He was never going to hear the end of this. He'd kidnapped a complete stranger, rescued her in the dead of night, and was about to come home bonded. *My psi-mate.* He reached out to her telepathically, something made possible by their bond. *"Merek is coming to get us."*

"Good," Ria said, stepping from the bathroom fully clothed. "Because I'm starving, and I need a shower." She stood there looking like a child, not sure what to do with herself. Probably just as conflicted as he was.

Ty got out of bed and dressed without saying a word. He felt her eyes on him. They were psi-mates, but they hardly knew each other. Not to mention the fact he'd kidnapped her. It occurred to him she must have people she needed to contact. But how could he let her? He ran a hand through his hair and stepped into the bathroom. More to have a moment of privacy than anything else. He went to the sink and splashed water on his face.

What was he going to do? He couldn't keep his own psi-mate locked up, but he couldn't exactly let her go either. She was Sandarian military. His gut twisted at the cruel joke fate had played on him. He gripped the rim of the sink and looked at himself in the mirror. He couldn't stay in here forever, but he had no idea what to do next.

* * * *

Ria paced. The wood cabin was small and rustic. Oddly feminine curtains hung on the three windows. A small kitchenette, table, and an old couch was the extent of it. There was only the one room so she couldn't avoid looking at the bed. Their bonding had been everything she'd imagined. More even. When they touched, she forgot everything. Forgot he was supposed to be a dimwitted Curzan and a killer. She hadn't sensed evil in him. Fear descended upon her like a blanket. What if their bond caused her to lose all objectivity? What if she was bonded to a man who stood for everything she'd fought against? She'd left the military when she'd discovered how corrupt the emperor was. Could it be she was now tied to someone just as bad? Was their bond preventing her from seeing him clearly? She wrapped her arms around herself.

He interrupted her thoughts when he stepped back into the room.

They faced each other in silence.

Ty slipped his hands in his front pockets and cocked his head. Long bangs fell across his face, and she had an intense urge to brush them away. "Looks like we have a little problem, Red."

"You call this a little problem?"

He scanned her body from head to toe and back again. "You're not very big."

Rage flared. Why did every male feel the need to make stupid comments like that? "You're not exactly huge."

His laughter pissed her off even more. She spun around and headed for the door. His speed surprised her as he caught her arm and spun her around. And there it was. His touch fed her on some impossible level.

He backed her against the door. "You can't run any more than I can."

She knew he was right, but she wasn't going to give him the satisfaction of hearing her say it.

He nodded as though he understood. "How two people from such different worlds could bond is beyond me. The Mother Goddess has a sick sense of humor." His thumb caressed the still-healing scar on her arm sending little bolts of pleasure outward.

She swallowed a slight moan before he continued.

"I may not like who or what you are, and I suspect you feel the same about me, but you're safe here. I would never hurt you. You know that, right?"

Ria wanted to scream, "Why you?" She hated the fact that when he leaned in, she met his kiss openly. Pleasure flowed as thought ceased.

* * * *

Just as things were getting out of control, there was a knock at the door. Ria shoved Ty backward. He stumbled a step and gave her an exasperated look with a shrug of his shoulders. They were both trapped.

Ty waved a hand, and the door opened to Merek. The large man's eyes flicked from one to the other with a questioning look.

Ria's face burned, and she turned away as though looking for something. Of course, there was nothing for her to find. It was embarrassing to have a psi-mate she didn't know.

One thing was becoming clear. All friction between them stopped the moment they touched. All thoughts, questions, and fears vanished. Their bodies and psi were so perfectly meshed, there was no denying it. She took another step away from Ty.

"Everything all right here?" Merek asked.

"It's fine," Ty said over Ria's puff.

Merek scanned the room, his eyes stopping at the rumpled bed. Ria refused to meet his gaze and kicked herself for not at least throwing a blanket and pillow on the couch.

"Let me get my darts, and we can head out," Ty said.

Ria watched him retrieve the weapons. They had been next to the bed the whole time. She'd never even considered trying to get one to use against him. He'd said he would never hurt her. But it was more—he *couldn't* hurt her. No more than she could hurt him.

She dropped her arms to her sides and met his gaze. *"This is an impossible situation."*

"And yet, here we are, Red."

Merek cleared his throat and motioned to the door. "Trin is worried sick about you."

Ria pushed her way past him and headed toward the cruiser. The sun warmed her skin. She climbed into the back seat and closed the door. She breathed a sigh of relief when Ty got into the front passenger seat. Merek reached out to the dashboard and grabbed a pair of psi-bands.

Ty turned to her. *"We don't need these anymore, do we?"*

"No." She wouldn't leave again until things were resolved one way or another. She leaned back and took in the forest around them.

Ty shook his head at Merek, and they made the trip back to the hunting lodge in silence.

The door to the lodge opened before the cruiser stopped and Bella bounded down the stairs. "Where have you guys been?" She gave a big hug to Ty, then turned to Ria and put her hands on her hips. "You promised."

It was impossible not to like the teen. "I know. I'm sorry. Don't worry, it won't happen again. See?" She held her hands out to emphasize there were no psi-bands.

"She's free?" Bella asked Ty.

"Well...she's got the run of the lodge."

"Thanks," she said to Ty. She'd always envied Dani and Ian being able to communicate like this, and it was cool. It just wasn't how she'd imagined it. *"I need to contact my people. Let them know I'm okay."* Sort of.

Ty's eyebrows drew together. *"I know. I'll see what I can do."*

Bella bounced on her heels next to Ria, presumably waiting for someone to say something. She gave up and grabbed Ria's arm. "Excellent. You not being locked up and all will give us more time to talk. Come on, you probably need a shower, and I washed your clothes for you." She chatted all the way up the stairs.

* * * *

Ty furrowed his brows as Bella ushered Ria off to her bedroom. Standing in the doorway to the lodge with her arms crossed was Trin. He climbed the stairs and stopped in front of her. "Sorry. I didn't have time to wake anyone."

"You best not let that happen again, mister. Family comes first, you hear?"

Inside Ria and Bella turned left at the top of the landing. She glanced down at him, and their connection buzzed. He wondered how long it would be before they were pulled together again. He turned his attention back to Trin. "Family first. I'm going to go clean up, and then we need to talk. Where's Olivia?"

"She's on a call with her dad. Ria's employer is pitching a fit over her disappearance." She stood on her toes and gave him a kiss on the cheek. "We'll talk about that, too, when you're back down. Now, go on with you."

Ty took the steps two at a time. Like it or not, his body was responding to having a psi-mate. He was energized and sensed her presence stronger than ever. He couldn't deny it felt good, but why her?

He showered quickly and went back downstairs with wet hair. Gathered around the dining room table were Merek, Trin, Bella, and Olivia. They'd turned it into a makeshift office while they worked on deciphering the old books.

Olivia came around the table the moment she saw him. "Are you nuts? Running off in the middle of the night?" She placed a hand on his arm and gave a gentle squeeze. He was going to have to break the news to her soon. Her touch had less-than-zero allure. Another side affect of being bonded.

She smiled, unaware. "My father would lock me up for a week if I pulled a stunt like that."

"I wouldn't recommend it. Tell me about your call. What's going on in Starfall?" He could tell she wanted more information about last night, but she answered, anyway.

"The Cavacent clan that Ria works for is making a lot of noise. Sou has your and Ria's pictures plastered on every vid and news feed on the planet. Rumors are flying about another crackdown on Curzans. My father's worried about the leaks in Watersedge. Especially Father Arlo. He can be tied to every Curzan that's died in the past two years."

"His church has a large congregation. Nearly a thousand people go to his services every week. He's not the only common denominator."

"He doesn't have to be," Olivia said quietly. "Rumor is that certain schools and churches are going to be targeted. They're going to spot-check DNA."

Gods, that would be a disaster. Last he heard, Arlo's church only had fifteen to twenty percent Mitans. The vast majority were Curzan. Nearly everyone who attended was complicit with their activities to help Curzans.

"All the more reason," Merek said, "to get a breakthrough on these texts. If we can prove native Curzans had psi, the GTO will have to return the planet to our rule."

It wouldn't be that easy. The Mitans had lived here for generations. It wouldn't be fair to kick the Mitans out just as it wasn't fair that the Curzans *possibly* had their planet illegally taken away from them. They still didn't know for sure. All they did know was that many Curzans had psi now. No, he thought their better option was to get rid of Mortog. Sou was a simpleton, and there were no other officials with Mortog's collective power. There was too much infighting among the city and town leaders for an immediate coup. If they took out Mortog, it could very well give them the time they needed to start recognizing Curzan equality. Ignoring the fact that Curzans had psi and killing them was punishable by GTO law. Not many were willing to risk such retribution the way Mortog was. The chancellor was the key. He needed to go. Olivia and her father agreed with Ty on this, but he was fairly sure Merek and Trin wouldn't go along with it.

In the meantime, deciphering the texts was the next most important thing they could do.

"There's one thing we need to discuss," Ty said. "It may help the situation with Sou and most certainly Ria's clan."

"What is it?" Merek asked.

"She needs to contact her people. Assure them she's okay and not being ill-treated."

"And then what?" Olivia snarled. "Give her the run of the place? Why don't we just let her play with the texts?"

Ria chose that moment to make an appearance at the top of the stairs.

"About that," Ty said.

"What is she doing loose?" Olivia jumped to her feet and drew her laser.

"Put it away," Ty said.

Ria walked down the stairs, head held high with a pissed off expression on her face. "I'm not your dog to be tied up and locked in a room."

"Why you—"

Ty grabbed Olivia as she lunged for Ria. He wasn't sure who was in need of protection at the moment.

Merek positioned himself between the two women as an added layer.

"Hold on, Olivia. Calm down. I told her she wasn't going to be locked up any more."

"Why in the name of the Goddess would you do that? She's Sandarian military. In case you forgot, they kill our people like it's a blasted sport."

Ty had no answer for that. She was right. Was he doing the right thing? Was he blinded by their bond?

"I don't kill Curzans," Ria said. "At least... not yet."

"That's quite enough," Merek said. "Ria, you sit there, please." He motioned to a chair next to Bella who sat open-mouthed. "Olivia, please take a seat over there."

Olivia growled but took a seat as far away from Ria as she could.

"Now"—Merek looked to Ty—"you care to tell us why we're suddenly letting our hostage, one you kidnapped as you'll recall, run around freely?"

Ty was surprised to find that Trin was fiddling with her set of knitting needles and smiling. *She knows.* He took a deep breath. "I can't lock her up."

"Why the *frack* not?" Olivia said.

He would have preferred to tell her in private, but that wasn't going to happen. "Because she's my psi-mate."

Bella squealed. Trin let her grin grow into a full-blown smile.

"Yep, I thought that might be the case." Merek rubbed the back of his neck and sat hard next to Trin who patted his shoulder.

Olivia glared at him, as if waiting for him to take it back.

Chapter 12

Going through the deceased Jara's files, it didn't take Sou long to find the young new informant. A mere teen named Connor. Jara had to find a new mole when he'd accidentally beaten the last one beyond the healers' ability to fix. Sou sent an undercover to pick him up and bring him to the PR's Palace. Mortog had created a delightful little space where they could conduct interviews of a certain nature without interruption. The boy lay on an inclined rack with his wrists and ankles pinned.

Mortog watched from behind one-way glass. Unable to communicate telepathically, Sou wore a small com clip in one ear. The fact that Mortog didn't show his face meant that the teen needed to live. A pity really. Sou enjoyed watching as bodies gasped for their last breath. After Sou smashed his left kneecap, the teen started talking.

"I'll ask you again before I crush your other knee, who is the leader in Watersedge?"

Connor's face was badly bruised and his upper lip split, but he still managed to answer. "Farther Arlo." His head fell forward.

"Oh, why so glum? You've already betrayed your fellow Curzans. What's a few more?"

The boy shot him daggers.

"There's one more thing I need before I get the healers and give you some relief. You'd like that, wouldn't you? Ease the pain?" Sou waited, but the boy didn't reply. He slapped the boy's broken knee, enjoying his response. "I want you to tell me about the texts."

Connor shook his head but didn't meet his eyes. Sou punched him in the face. Never more alive than when he inflicted pain on others, he laughed with the feeling of power.

The boy looked up, blood now flowing freely from his lip. "I don't know about any texts."

"You lie! Jara reported to me. Tell me about the texts that will 'change everything.' Those were his exact words. What was he talking about?"

Tears rolled down the youth's face. It made Sou want to hit him again. He pulled his hand back, but Connor finally talked.

"It may be nothing. They don't know. They're ancient texts. Merek is sure they'll prove Curzans had psi when Salvator took the planetary rulership."

It was difficult to make out his words, but the meaning was clear.

Sou moved to strike again when Mortog's voice stopped him. "Enough. Summon the healers and come here."

In the next room Sou found Mortog pacing.

"You must find those texts. They need to be destroyed." He reached into a pocket and handed a coin-sized device to Sou.

"What is this?"

"A tracking device. Have the healers insert it into the boy's body."

"But, sir. The underground will surely scan for that."

"Ah, this is a unique device. The same engineers that developed our beloved psi-bands recently came up with this. It is completely organic and will not transmit, and therefore can't be detected until remotely activated. Send the boy to Father Arlo. He must tell the priest that a massive sweep is imminent."

"How would he know this?"

"I don't know, and I don't care." Mortog leaned in, inches from Sou's face. "Make it work. When you lose them—because you always do, don't you?—I'll activate the device and we'll have our Watersedge Underground."

* * * *

"It's been almost a week, Ian. Where the hell is she?" Dani pulled her blond hair. It was a bad habit she had when she needed to clear her head.

"I don't know." Ian paced nearby. They were staying at Darl's place again since the portal was still open. Officially, they wouldn't arrive until the transport ship they were supposedly on did, and that wasn't for another day.

They'd been here for two days and gotten no closer to finding Ria or Ty Sordina. Sou's men were useless, and something was nagging Dani, but she couldn't figure out what it was. Maybe it was just Sou. She didn't like him.

"I know Sou said they'd checked everything, but we can't just sit here. I say we do our own research, starting with Ty's family."

"Works for me." Ian grabbed his com and held the door for her and Armond.

"Wait a moment," Armond said. He dug around his duffle bag and pulled out a small case. Inside were focal points. Small round devices that could be used to pinpoint their location and activate an emergency portal move. They'd saved the lives of Dani, Ian, Ria, and Balastar back on Sandaria. "If I'd given one of these to Ria, we never would have lost her. It was my oversight."

It was difficult to feel sympathy for the arrogant albino. "It's not your fault she was kidnapped," Dani said. "We had no way of knowing she was in any danger."

"Even so. Please do not go anywhere without one on you."

Ian slipped the small device into his pocket. "This is standard equipment from now on."

"Yes, sir," Armond said.

The ride to the Sordina's small home took less than ten minutes. It was a pretty place sitting on an unpaved road a few hundred yards off a minor access route into town. Tall trees blocked the view of the road but once they stood on the front porch, which overlooked the treetops, it was beautiful. The water in the bay sparkled in the late morning sun and the northern cliffs were visible in the distance. An intricately carved wooden plaque hung next to the door. *Sordina Woodworkers. Please Come In.*

Ian pulled the screen door open, and Dani stepped inside. The entire bottom floor was a woodworking shop. It smelled of fresh wood and acidic varnish.

The sound of footsteps descending from above told them they weren't alone. Dani hoped it was Ty's mother or father. An older man came down the stairs. He had gray hair, a kind face, and a bulbous nose. From the look of his robes, he was a priest of some kind. He carried a large burlap sack and halted the moment he saw them. "Good day, brethren. May the Mother Goddess smile upon you."

"And you, Father," Ian said stepping forward to shake the man's hand. "Are you Mr. Sordina?"

"No, no. I'm Father Arlo, but please, just Arlo. I'm here to take care of the place for them." He paused a moment to look at each of them. "I assume you've heard about the boy, Ty?"

"That's why we're here," Dani said, stepping forward to introduce herself. Armond followed suit.

"Ah." The priest set down the bag and shook his finger at them. "You're the EPs. From the Cavacent clan, yes? You captured Ty."

Dani told Ian, *"He doesn't feel hostile. More like hopeful."*

"That's correct," Ian said, not offering anything further.

"I didn't realize you were back on Mitah. But of course you would be with one of yours missing."

"That's right." Again, Ian kept his response to a minimum.

The priest was agitated. He tapped his fingers together, then seemed to make up his mind about something. "Do you have a moment?"

"Do you know something about Ria?" Dani couldn't stop herself.

Arlo frowned. "Yes and no." He held a finger to his lips. He went to the front door and peeked out, looking left and right before securing the deadbolt. "Please, follow me."

He led them to the back of the shop and out onto a porch. He kept his voice low. "How much do you know, if you don't mind my asking."

Dani looked to Ian who gave her the go-ahead. "We know that Ty killed a high-ranking security official. We know that Ty is a Curzan, not the Mitan he pretended to be. And we know he kidnapped Ria."

"Yes, yes. All true. But as is so often the case, the truth is multifaceted." He paused again. "I have no idea why he took your EP, but I can assure you, she's safe."

"He killed a man in cold blood," Dani said.

Arlo's fingers were interwoven, and he flexed them repeatedly. "Leon Jara was not a good being. That does not excuse Ty, but there are many who wish they'd done the deed."

"That's not enough to convince me she's all right," Ian said.

"I'm quite sure she's fine."

Armond who'd stood silently watching the proceedings, spoke up. "You know this to be fact." It wasn't a question.

"I do," Arlo said, quietly, scanning the forest around them.

"How?" Dani asked. "How do you know?"

"Let's just say, I've heard things."

"Where is she?" Dani said. "We need to talk to her."

"I don't know where she is, just that she is well enough."

"Look," Ian said, stepping inches away from the priest, "we're not going to play games with you. How do we find her?"

"I assure you these are not games. They are, in fact, a matter of life and death. Ty has started something that isn't going to end well. Not without help from the outside."

"Outside?" Ian asked.

"Outside of our government on Mitah. It is no secret that your father is very powerful and has connections in the GTO. I beg you to get a message to him. It is fairly clear that the Curzans on this planet, psi-abled

Curzans"—he raised his eyebrows to emphasize the point—"face imminent mass genocide unless someone can stop Chancellor Mortog."

"That is no small accusation, Father."

For the next ten minutes, the priest told them of a series of murders that had occurred at an increasing pace. Finally, he got to the old man, Jafferies, who Darl had investigated.

"We heard about Jafferies," Dani said. "He'd lived here a long time."

"Over thirty years. In peace. He was dying a slow, painful death from a malady that is easily cured in Mitan med centers. But he wasn't Mitan, you see. So he could not get treatment."

"They don't give Curzans access to meds?" Ian asked.

"Only if their owners provide the necessary paperwork. As a Mitan, he had no owner and DNA testing is standard procedure for everyone. He would have been found out."

"Oh God, Ian. This is getting worse and worse." Dani wanted to take her psi-mate's hand but kept still.

"Curzans are not the near animals you've been led to believe. Many of them, although not all, have psi, and they are every bit as intelligent as any Mitan. Education is denied them, as is basic freedom. It has been thus for so long, it is ingrained into the culture on this planet. Many are opening their eyes and seeing the truth, but Mortog wants nothing to do with equality."

"My father isn't as powerful as Arlo seems to think," Ian said to her.

"He's friends with Supreme Commander, Torril Anantha. That's more power than most people."

"And the GTO's resourses are already spread too thin. Mitah may throw a nice ball once a year, but it has little or no other significance."

"We have to try to help."

Ian nodded. "I'll contact my father, but don't get your hopes up. I don't know how much we can do."

"It's a start. Thank you."

"Arlo," Dani said, "are you a Curzan?"

"No. I simply recognized the injustice from a young age. I've spent my life making a safe place for them to live and grow. I fear it is all falling apart."

"You should be safe though, right?" Dani asked.

"I'm afraid not. If Sou or any of his people find out how much I've done for the Curzans, my life will be forfeit."

Dani made up her mind. "I don't know how, but we're going to help you."

"I felt it would be worth the risk to talk to you. I'm glad I was right."

"Can you get a message to Ria?" Ian asked.

"Eventually. I never know when or where I will be contacted. The Starfall Underground is hiding them, along with those that live here in this house."

"Tell them about us," Dani said on impulse.

"Dani, don't make promises you can't keep."

She gave the love of her life a scathing look.

"Okay, okay." Ian raised his hands. "We'll do everything we can."

The priest smiled at the two. It was an honest, kind smile.

Chapter 13

Ria delicately turned a page of the ancient handwritten journal she and Bella were working on. An uneasy truce had settled over the occupants of the lodge. Everyone but Trin was gathered around the table, poring over the mysterious texts. Ria shared Bella's fascination with the journal and spent most of her time on it.

Olivia sat next to Ty, cross-referencing a notebook and one of the many texts.

Ria was bothered by Olivia's proximity to Ty. The fact she was bothered by it also annoyed her. She frowned at the pair and twirled a strand of red hair around her finger.

Since she and Ty had bonded the day before, they'd kept their distance. It wasn't a perfect pairing by any stretch. They should be talking, getting to know each other, but she didn't know how to do that when there was so much distrust between them. One thing was clear. It was getting harder to stay apart. She knew from her experience with Dani and Ian that she and Ty couldn't stay away forever. Soon the tension and desire would bring them together again whether they wanted it or not. She was torn between anger and anticipation.

The notebook Ty had created was full of possible keys to the language they labored over. Ria wasn't sure she could have produced such a thing. He caught her looking at him, and she quickly pulled her hand away from her hair.

"That's really impressive." She said, nodding at the note pad.

He looked at her a moment and put his pen down before leaning back in his chair with arms crossed. "Did you think I couldn't do something like this?"

"That's not what I meant." She didn't appreciate his tone.

"I suppose you've heard that Curzans lack intelligence."

"Yeah, I heard that." She leaned forward on her elbows. What was his problem? "Intelligence and morals," she said, getting really pissed now.

"You want to talk about lacking morals?" Ty slammed his hands on the table. He clipped a pen that flew into the air and landed with a clatter on the floor.

Olivia glared at Ria while she reached down and retrieved the pen. When she handed it to Ty, she brushed his fingers.

It was a provocative motion and the jealousy that flared sent Ria over the edge. "Okay, let's talk morals. Why don't we start with the morality of kidnapping?"

"Oy." Merek leapt to his feet and took Ria's upper arm, pulling her to a stand. "I think I hear Trin calling from the kitchen. I'm sure she could use some help." He practically dragged her down the hall. "You two with your tempers." He shook his head when they were out of sight.

"All I said was that key he's working on was impressive." Ria pulled her arm away but kept in step with him. The anger slid away. "I'm sorry, Merek. I shouldn't have made that comment about morals. Curzans aren't what they're made out to be."

"No, we're not." He stopped just inside the kitchen. "I'm glad you can see that for yourself."

Trin turned to see what was going on.

"I'm not kidding about your temper," Merek said. "Ty's is bad enough. We can't have both of you going off." He rubbed the back of his neck and shook his head. "This is like no bonding I've ever heard of. That's the truth. Stay here. Help Trin. And, please, try not to set him off."

She wanted to point out that it hadn't been her fault. She'd complimented the man, for frack's sake. But Merek wasn't looking at her with anger or malice. It was more of a helpless frustration.

"Go on," Trin said to her husband. "And take this with you. These should calm him down." She plucked a plate of cookies off the counter and waited for Ria to take one before handing it to Merek.

After he was gone, Ria took a bite. "Hm, that's really good."

"Thank you, dear."

"You're a good mom." Ria smiled at her, but Trin didn't return the look.

"I'm not his biological mother."

"But, I thought—"

"You thought what you were supposed to think." She wiped her hands on the dishtowel she was holding and placed it on the counter. "You want to know why he hates Sandarian military so much?"

Ria wasn't entirely sure she did, but if it helped her understand him, it was worth a shot. She took another bite and simply nodded.

"It was just over fifteen years ago now. Ty's folks were secretly schooling the Curzan children in the woods."

"Why secretly?"

"Because Curzans are forbidden to learn, to educate themselves."

The cookie went dry in her mouth. She didn't want to ask the question but had to. "What happened?"

"That man he killed at the ball, Leon Jara? He killed Ty's parents in front of the class they were teaching. In front of him. It was almost an hour before the other Curzan parents showed up to collect their kids and found the carnage."

Ria's stomach churned. She thought back to the morning she and Ty bonded, and knew, without a doubt, the faces she'd seen were his parents.

"Jara recently returned from another stint in your beloved military," Trin continued. "They say he picked up where he left off where Curzans were concerned."

Ria chaffed at the term "beloved military," but the extent to which these people had been repressed made her ill. Earth had plenty history of entire peoples slaughtered or enslaved. Her gut dropped as she imagined a young Ty hovering over the lifeless bodies of his parents. Anger boiled, and she knew she would have done the same thing. *Oh, Ty. We need to start over. Neither of us are what the other thought.* She had to try to help. Surely, Rucon could do something?

"I left the military when I discovered it was as corrupt as our emperor," Ria said, needing to explain, however little. "They're turning things around now. Weeding out those who don't value basic rights and liberties. I know because I have friends still there. Friends who wanted to stick it out and make a difference. They didn't bail, like me."

Trin took Ria's hand. "There's no shame in not doing what you know is wrong, child. What is a shame is what's going on with you and Ty right now. You two are never going to be able to stay apart for long. This relationship needs fixing. I know there's a lot of anger in him, but there's a lot of love to be had there, too." She squeezed Ria's hand and let it go. "Now come on, help me with dinner."

Ria stayed in the kitchen another hour. She needed the time to process what Trin had said. She couldn't deny the fluttering in her stomach at the mention of love. Ty was starting to make sense, which was kind of nice since nothing else about this situation did.

During dinner, Ty sat as far away as possible. It wasn't working any longer, however, and they both knew it. Neither of them could hold still, and every time their eyes met by chance, a thrill bolted through her core. She was losing it. She needed the feel of his skin on hers. She tried to put a stop to the thoughts, but it was no use. She rose abruptly and made some excuse about not feeling well. Strictly speaking, it was true. She took her plate to the kitchen and set it in the sink. She sensed Ty a moment before he placed his hands on her hips and turned her around.

She met his kiss without a word. They didn't need words. She was ready to let him take her then and there when, thank the Gods, he pulled away.

He placed a hand on her face, his thumb trailing along her cheekbone. He shook his head. *"Your room or mine?"*

"Whichever is closer."

He took her hand and led her out the kitchen and, thankfully, away from the dining room. She couldn't stand the thought of traipsing past everyone. She would though, if that was what it took to get him alone. They'd waited long enough. Stopping now wasn't an option. They went down a poorly lit passage and up a narrow flight of stairs.

"It's an old servants' passage," he said to her. *"Never thought I'd be using it like this."*

She felt his humor. *"I appreciate the detour."*

He turned right at the top of the stairs. Of course, he'd selected the room farthest from hers. Closing the door behind them, he pulled her into his arms and pressed her against his hard chest. All the tension during the last few days, their inability to talk, the distrust, disintegrated in one passionate kiss. Her last thought before letting go completely was *I can fix this.*

Their psi burned in a frenzy. Ria buzzed with energy like drinking too much caff. She needed this man, and she needed him now. Reaching up, she ripped his shirt open, sending buttons flying. His eyes burned with gray light as he yanked her shirt up over her head. They fumbled out of their shoes and the rest of their clothes before coming together again. Skin on skin, the heat of his body fed something deep inside her as she met his kiss. He tasted of the spiced wine from dinner. The way he smelled, of spice and forest, intoxicated her.

More.

She pushed him backward toward the bed. He slid back to the center of the mattress and she followed. Crouching low, she bit and nibbled her way from his ankle to his thigh. She ran her hands up and down his legs, drunk with desire.

He propped himself up on his elbows and spread his legs wider.

When their eyes locked, she held his gaze as their connection ignited. Her breath expelled as the intense pleasure ripped through her. When she couldn't take anymore, she looked down. His erection pulsed when she wrapped her hand around it. Hot and hard, it beckoned with the promise of more pleasure. No—of ecstasy. She bent and licked the tip, smearing the precum around her lips. She took him into her mouth then, wetting his shaft and taking as much as she could before sliding her lips up and down. Wetting her palm on her saliva and his juice, she pumped him in rhythm with her mouth.

Ty reached down and wrapped his fingers through her hair. He pulled to the brink of pain as he moved with her. "Baby, your mouth is magic."

She had to agree. Their connection made it possible for her to experience some of what he did. It was her mouth and hand, and yet somehow she felt it between her legs. Nearing the brink, she stopped. In one swift motion, he flipped her onto her back. He hovered over her, breathing hard.

The mix of passion and anger they stirred in each other had her growling as she pulled him down for a kiss. His tongue probed and searched her. Her growl turned to a whimper as he melted her core.

She squirmed, rubbing her aching clit against his cock.

"Gods, fuck me, Ty."

She lifted her knees and locked her ankles around his waist as he slammed into her. Pounding her into an oblivion they both desperately needed. The tension in their bodies and psi rose together. Faster and higher they climbed until they crested.

Ria heard her own voice cry out as the pleasure blasted through them. An explosion that rocketed through her body and consumed her psi. She let it pulse, and then lowered her shaking legs as Ty's body came to rest next to her.

She drifted back to herself slowly as Ty trailed his fingers between her breasts. She opened her eyes to find him propped on one elbow looking at her.

His face was a mask. She had no idea what to say. Where to start. He scanned her body and ran his free hand everywhere it could reach.

It felt so good.

He found each breast in turn, toying with her nipples before running his hand up her neck and rubbing his thumb across her lips.

The gesture so tender, so loving… She nearly cried as she reached up and cupped his face with her palm.

Gods, but this man was gorgeous. His eyes were back to their normal color, and no doubt hers were, as well. He didn't avoid her gaze, which was odd after days of keeping their distance.

He reached over and tucked her hair behind her ear. "You are the most beautiful thing I have ever seen."

The sentiment and sincerity took her breath away. "The feeling is mutual." She desperately wanted to trace his surprisingly red lips, but she didn't. "Ty..." She stared into his eyes. How could they be so close and so far apart?

A lopsided grin formed across those amazing lips. "You're going to tell me we need to talk, aren't you?"

He was teasing her, and it felt good. Virtually everything about him was foreign to her. "You know me well."

"No." He sat up, and she did the same, sitting cross-legged facing him. He stretched his legs out on either side of her, lightly placing his hands on her knees.

His touch had the butterflies in her stomach going crazy.

"I don't know you well. I don't know you at all, Red. I have a hard time reconciling what we are together and what you are, or were, before."

It was a huge understatement. "Promise me something?"

"What?"

"Right here, right now, we'll be totally honest with each other. We can't go on like we've been. I don't want to go on like that."

He took her hand and rubbed his thumb around her palm.

Tendrils of delight snaked up her wrist.

"I don't either, but I'm not sure if complete honesty is really what you want."

She didn't even think about it. "It's what I need."

Ty grinned. He had a sinful, delicious smile that grabbed her heart. "What you need is me."

She nodded. "True. But I need all of you. Not just this." She leaned forward and kissed him deeply.

He pulled on her bottom lip with his teeth when he leaned back. "What changed, Red? Why aren't you fighting this anymore?"

"When I was helping Trin in the kitchen earlier, she told me...about your parents." His pain rippled through her.

He rubbed his temples. "So now you know."

She put a hand on his shoulder, gripping hard. "We're not all like that."

"I know, Ria. But you're the worst kind. Tell me I'm wrong, and you're not ex-military."

His words ruffled, but she reminded herself of why he felt the way he did. "You're not wrong. I was in the military. But I got out as soon as I could, once I realized how deep the corruption was." She struggled to find the words, wanting him to understand completely. "You should know that I'd still be serving, with pride, if it had been the kind of force it was meant to be. I believe in the need for a military to protect its citizens and keep the peace." She trailed her fingers down his muscled arms. "That's how I found my way to the Cavacent clan. They're honest and decent people. And as for the military, things are getting better now, Ty. I know. I have friends that are still serving."

"Gods woman," Ty said, pulling at her thighs and placing her legs on either side of him. His erection made thinking a difficult prospect. He put his hands on her ass and lifted her onto his lap.

He studied her face a moment. "I wish I could believe you."

Ria placed her palms on his chest. "You don't believe me?" Anger flared.

"Relax. You said to be honest. I believe that you believe what you're saying. We're making a start here. You're going to have to give me some time." His eyes flashed and his erection sparked another fire between her legs.

"Promise we'll talk and stop avoiding each other?"

"If we did that, we'd end up here a lot more often." He lifted her up and slowly impaled her. She closed her eyes and let the pleasure build. "I think I could handle that."

It was a start. She wouldn't let them stay apart again. She understood his anger toward her now and knew he wasn't the killer she'd thought. He was her psi-mate, and she wanted to know everything about him.

In time. Thought stopped as the rhythm of their bodies took over.

Chapter 14

Rain pelted Ty's face as he ran. The familiar feeling of dread filled him. Thunder exploded overhead, and he instinctively ducked. They ducked. She was with him. She was always with him. They had to get to safety. The cache! There was a weapons cache hidden in those cliffs. They would be safe if they could just get a little farther. She cried out, and he turned to find her kneeling on the boulders behind him. He spun around to help her up, and they ran to the fissure in the cliff face. Panic filled him. He knew what was coming but was powerless to stop it. "We're almost there." He reached back to pull her in when a laser tore through her body. "No!"

Ty bolted upright. Ria shot up next to him, a bead of sweat sliding down her cheek. She'd had the dream, too. He wrapped her in his arms and lay back against the pillows, heart still pounding.

"Why do we keep having that dream," Ria said, curling in closer to his chest.

"I don't know. It started after you took me down at the Summer's Ball."

"Me, too."

"We'll just make sure we stay away from any cliff faces." Telling her about the cache wouldn't serve any purpose. He peered down into her green eyes. He'd been an idiot to try to keep his distance. He believed in her sincerity when she had talked about the military last night. He toyed with her silky hair. She didn't strike him as naïve. Maybe, just maybe, she was right about the change in the military. For their sake and that of the empire, he hoped so.

His stomach rumbled.

"Hungry?" She traced her fingers along his chest.

"Starving." He took a deep breath of her intoxicating scent and knew he could spend the rest of his life staring into those eyes of hers.

A slight crease wrinkled her brow.

"What is it?" He asked.

"Are we okay?"

He couldn't keep her at arm's length anymore if he wanted to. "We're better than okay. We're psi-mates. I want to know everything about you. From the day you were born until the moment I swept you off your feet."

"Gods," Ria laughed. "Is that what you call kidnapping?"

"Strictly speaking, I did sweep you off your feet." They both laughed then. Happiness unlike anything he thought possible swelled inside, and he vowed to spend the rest of his days finding ways to make her laugh. He wanted her again, would always want her, but they needed to get downstairs. Warder Zar's underground was supposed to have contacted Arlo last night. He needed to know if everything was all right. While they dressed, he filled Ria in on the collective underground and the rumors of DNA testing.

"He will kill them. Women, children, all of them. You understand," he finally said, "Mortog must be stopped."

"I know. We need to get the GTO to step in. It may take time, but I'm sure they'll help."

He'd just pulled his shirt on when he paused to look at her. She was used to following orders. Of course, she'd assume they'd try to work within the system. "We both know the GTO isn't going to care about screwed up politics on Mitah."

Her beautiful face paled. "Ty, you can't just kill him."

He didn't answer. He could, and he would, as soon as they had a plan.

She stood in front of him and grabbed his shirt, twisting it as she pulled him closer. "We just found each other. I am not letting *you* spend the rest of *our* lives in jail. Promise me you won't kill him."

Frack. He wrapped his arms around her and held her tight. *"I can't promise you that, my love."*

Ria pushed back and shoved him with her psi.

He stumbled backward a few steps. "Ria, wait, please. I'm being honest with you. You said that's what you wanted. I won't make a promise I may not be able to keep. I love you, Red. I'll do everything I can to keep us together. Forever. I promise. I don't want to fight anymore. Please." He opened his arms, and she came to him. He held her where she belonged for a long while until he felt her anger subside. "Come on. Let's go eat and find out what's going on in Watersedge." She wasn't happy with him, but she loved him. That was enough for now.

* * * *

Ria felt sucker punched. She couldn't let Ty kill the chancellor and be taken away from her. At best, he'd be locked up, at worst, he'd be killed. The very thought was enough to shake her.

He took her hand and kissed it as they headed downstairs. *"I love you, Red."* He shot her that grin that melted her insides every time.

"I love you, too. You'd better keep your ass alive for me."

Her face flushed as they entered the kitchen. Everyone was there, and they all stared at them. She tried to pull her hand away, but Ty only held on tighter.

"Yay!" Bella squealed, clapping her hands. "We're like sisters-in-law now." The teen, already taller than Ria, came in for a big hug, forcing Ty to let her go.

Trin and Merek joined them.

"About time," Merek said, clapping Ty on the back.

"I knew you two would be okay," Trin said.

Ria caught a pained look on Olivia's face as she walked out of the kitchen. She glanced at Ty who'd noticed as well. He brushed his psi across hers. There was no doubting his love for her, but the thought of him being with another woman made her insanely jealous.

Merek shrugged as he watched Olivia walk down the hall. "Why don't you two grab some plates and meet us in the dining room. Olivia was about to fill us in on Warder's contact with Arlo."

"Sounds good," Ty said.

They got their food, and Trin joined them in the dining room.

"How is Olivia communicating with her dad without being traced?" Ria asked Ty.

"She gets a new com every few days and only uses them once. Everything is coded. It's not perfect, but the chances of being intercepted are slim."

In the dining room, Olivia was all business.

"What's the status?" Merek asked as Ria and Ty sat down to eat.

It made Ria ridiculously happy when Ty sat next to her instead of the other end of the table.

"Our underground contacted Arlo around ten p.m. last night. He had news. He was at your home yesterday, Merek, gathering the clothes you requested and came in contact with Ria's fellow EPs."

Ria dropped her fork. "Ian? There wasn't any trouble, was there?"

"Quite the contrary," Olivia said. "Father Arlo basically pleaded our case. Ian promised to take it to his father and see what they could do."

"I told you," Ria said. "I'm sure Rucon will be able to do something to help."

Ty shared a look with Olivia that had her blood boiling. Which in turn made her angry with herself. She wasn't some insecure, jealous child. "Olivia, you have to let us try and help you. Taking out the chancellor on your own isn't going to do anything but get you in trouble."

"What we, as Curzans, choose to do is none of your business," Olivia snapped.

"It is now," Ria said.

"All right, you two." Merek held a hand up. "Ria's right. She's on our side now."

Olivia fumed, but remained silent.

"What else did Arlo say?" Merek asked.

"There have been no further developments. My father warned Arlo about the rumors. He suggested that the priest lock up the church and leave."

"The entire congregation can't just leave," Ty said.

"We know that. But with the church closed, they won't be so easily found." She chewed the inside of her cheek. "One more thing. A number of rooms at our headquarters are freeing up over the next two days. Dad would like you guys to relocate there. We're getting closer to gaining access to Mortog and may need to strike quickly."

"Ty. You can't," Ria said.

He didn't answer her, just gave her leg a squeeze under the table.

Olivia glared at her. "If they test DNA in the schools and churches of Watersedge, how long do you think it will be until they start finding Curzans? Do you want to take responsibility for the death of hundreds? Because here on Mitah, that's the punishment for impersonating a Mitan."

"She's right. We don't have time for diplomacy."

Ria glanced around the table. She'd stepped into a battle they'd been fighting all their lives. The empire was a different place now, changing, but it wasn't going to be fast enough for these people. "I want to talk to Ian."

Olivia started to protest, but Ty stopped her. "Give me one of your coms. I'll take her far away from here and let her make the call. I'll destroy the com and return. We'll stay below the tree line. It won't take long."

* * * *

Twenty minutes later, she and Ty were touching down on the edge of the Trillion Forest.

"Can I ask you a question?" Ria turned to face him.

"Of course."

"Olivia seems pretty upset. Did you and her... Is there a history I should know about?"

Ty turned the com over in his hand. "We've both made freeing Curzans a priority in our lives, but yes, our paths crossed a few times."

Ria hated the way that made her feel. Truth was, under normal circumstances she'd probably like the woman.

"You're not worried, are you?" Ty stroked her hair. "We're bonded. For life."

"I'm not worried, exactly. I just hate the thought of you with someone else. At least I understand where she's coming from now."

Ty handed her the com.

"I want my own back. It had personality."

"Your com?"

"Yeah." Ria smiled at the thought. "It had settled on the persona of an English butler, accent and all."

Ty raised an eyebrow at her.

"Which means nothing whatsoever to you. I'll show you when I get it back."

"Sorry, Merek ditched it after clobbering you over the head." Ty gave her a soul-searching look. "That seems so long ago, but it's only been a few days." He trailed his fingers along her jaw. "Make it quick and no names."

Ria sent a communication request to Ian's com. He wouldn't recognize this device so she added an identifier that would make him take notice. *Snow White.*

"Who is this?" Ian said.

"You know who it is. I can't talk long. All communicators on this planet are open to interception. I'm okay. Great, actually. The person you met last night spoke the truth. These people are in trouble. The person at the top is planning something that could cost dozens, maybe hundreds, of innocent lives. He has to be stopped."

"We're working on it. Are you safe?"

"For now. We don't have much time."

"We?"

"They're my people now, too."

Ty caressed her with his psi. *"Times up."*

"I have to go. I'll be in touch as soon as I can. Trust the priest and those he's working with." Ria disconnected and handed the device over to Ty. He got out of the cruiser and tossed the com to the ground before aiming his laser. Within seconds, the device was a molten pile of plastic and metal. Covering it with dirt, he returned to the cruiser and they went back to the lodge.

When they entered, they found the others hovering over the table in an excited state.

"You did it," Bella said, calling them over.

"What did you find?" Ty asked.

"You found it, boy." Merek picked up Ty's notes and waived them about. "The keys are matching up. We have a lot of words to identify, but the correlation is too high to be pure chance. We're on our way to reading these."

The excitement in the room was palpable. Trin beamed as she left the room for more drinks.

Ria joined Bella, and they started dissecting the journal. It was tedious and slow going but they figured out it belonged to a Curzan engineer. Things seemed to tumble into place after that, and they made good progress.

An hour later, the group was silent.

"I don't believe it," Ty said.

"We're not a hundred percent sure yet," Olivia said.

"It all fits." Bella tapped a notepad with her pen. "If this word means 'psi,' this is proof. Curzans had psi when this planet was deeded to Salvator."

"It's interesting, though," Merek said. "This implies that only some portion of the planet had psi. Perhaps that's why they were able to hide it. It would have been easy enough to pull from the non-psi segment for any verification."

Ty nodded. "A planet with a native population that was divided between those with psi and those without. That could be why they turned against each other."

"This is really important stuff," Ria said. "Not only does it mean some Curzans had psi, it means the whole population was suppressed from the first. You had nuclear power. Why hasn't anyone asked that question? If Curzans have such low intelligence, how could they have had such an advanced society? Think about that underground. That took advanced technology. The whole thing is appalling." Ria felt sick at the generations of Curzans struggling to make it here. "They had to know what they were doing. We need to get this in front of Supreme Commander Anantha. The GTO can sort this out."

"We'll work this from every angle." Merek rubbed his hands together. "We photograph and document what we need for proof. Do you think Rucon Cavacent can get this to the GTO Commander?"

"I'm sure he can," Ria said.

"We should do more than that." Ty tapped the table.

"What are you thinking?" Trin entered the room with two pitchers of the lemonade-like drink that was favored on Mitah.

"We release a vid. Send it planet-wide."

"Can you do that?" Ria asked.

"We can try," Olivia said. "We have people in two of the major networks. They'll have to go underground afterward, but it could be worth it. We need to get back to our base. We can make the copies and record the vid there. I'll call my father and arrange for our return."

When Olivia returned, Ria was alone in the dining room. "They're upstairs packing."

"I should get my things, as well."

"Can you wait a sec?" Ria put the last journal into the box and closed the lid.

"What do you want?" Olivia eyed her suspiciously.

Ria stepped around the table and approached. "I want to apologize."

Olivia's eyebrows shot up.

"I've been a bitch, and you don't deserve it." Of course, Olivia had been a bitch, too, but she could understand why. "This thing with Ty... It really threw me. And I know you guys have some history. The thought of you with him made me crazy." She shoved her hands into her back pockets. "I'm sorry."

Olivia let out a heavy sigh. "You weren't the only bitch."

Ria smiled. "I was going to say that, but..."

Olivia laughed. "I can't believe you tried to escape in that forest with no repellers and no weapons."

"I can't believe you walked into the Starfall police station dressed as a security agent." Ria extended her hand. "Start over?"

"Sure."

They shook hands. Olivia was beautiful. Classic dark hair and skin. But Ty was hers now. There was no need for jealousy.

* * * *

Dani waited anxiously for Ian to finish the call. He'd signaled her as soon as he connected with Ria.

When he was done, he changed direction and walked back the way they'd come.

She whirled around and rushed to catch up. "Well? What did she say?"

He raised an eyebrow at her. "She said they were her people now."

"He *is* her psi-mate! Did she sound happy? Is she okay? Where are they?"

"Cease, woman." Ian teased.

"You did not just call me 'woman.'"

He blasted her with pleasure so intense she stumbled, but he caught her by the waist and kept her moving. Being psi-mates had its advantages.

"She couldn't talk long," he said, kissing the top of her head. "She sounded happy. I have no idea where they are. She said to trust the priest and the people he's working with. It's time we find out who those people are."

Night was falling, but the double moons shone bright in the sky and would keep it twilight for hours. They found Father Arlo in the back room of his church, packing a bag. He greeted them warmly when they entered. "Ah, excellent, I was going to call you when I was away from here. The underground contacted me last night. I told them about you, and they wish to meet."

"Good," Ian said. "We just heard from Ria, and we'd like to meet with them, as well."

The priest stopped what he was doing. "She contacted you?"

"It was a brief call, but yes."

"And she is well?"

Dani snorted. "More than well from what we understand."

Arlo looked confused but resumed packing. "I'm glad to hear it. I don't know what that boy was thinking when he took her."

"I do." Dani swung her arms back and forth. *"I can't wait to talk to her and get the story."*

Ian cleared his throat. "He probably didn't either. Are you leaving for good?"

"Gods forbid," Arlo said. "There are some disturbing rumors circulating. The underground felt it best to disappear and close the church for a time." His grief was palpable. "It is not my choice, but I fear for the safety of my congregation. If you would come with me, I'm meeting with my contact. Perhaps we can arrange your introduction."

"Sounds good."

"Is it just you two? Where is your tall friend?"

"He's researching on his own." They'd decided to keep Armond back at Darl's place. He'd be near the portal if anything happened and more able to assist.

"You should call your dad," Dani said. "Let him know our plans."

Ian nodded and stepped aside to call his father. He was back a moment later. "That's the second message I've left." He addressed the priest. "Would you excuse us a moment? We'll be right back."

"Of course. I'll finish packing and lock up."

"What are we doing?" Dani asked.

"Checking in with Armond. I'm worried about my father." Ian led the way outside and around the side of the church. *"Get your focal point and leave it on the ground here."*

She dropped the tiny device and took his hand before he pressed his own focal point. A moment later, they found themselves standing next to a puzzled-looking Armond.

"Is something wrong?" Armond stood to greet them.

"Possibly," Ian said. "Have you seen my father since yesterday?"

"No, I have not."

That ruled out his using the portal. "Has anyone used the portal since we got here?"

"No. It is not like your father to be unresponsive."

"As of now, he is to be considered missing. Contact our Captain at the spaceport and see if he's heard or seen anything."

"Tell him about Ria," Dani said, anxious to get back to the priest.

"She called me," Ian said. "She's safe for now. Dani and I are going to meet with the people that have her. It sounds like they aren't the bad guys in this scenario. She said coms aren't secure on Mitah. From now on, assume you're being listened to. I want you to take the portal back to Earth and explain to my mother what's going on. She needs to contact Supreme Commander Anantha. He and my father are close. She'll have his number. She needs to impress upon him that the acting PR is corrupt, a large population of psi-abled beings are about to be murdered and Rucon is missing."

"Yes, sir."

"Do you have an ETA for Balastar?"

"They should be arriving on Earth in approximately four hours."

"Good. Stay there until they arrive, then come back with Marco. Leave the portal open so I can contact you if needed. And make sure Mordo stays there. We should not have left Earth without a direct descendant. We should not have risked our clan being stranded on Earth without a leader and without rights."

"Mordo will not wish to stay behind."

"I know. Repeat what I just said to him. He should see the truth of it."

"I will see it done. I will also make sure everyone has a focal point from now on."

"Good. What's the ETA of our second ship? We can't make ourselves known to the authorities until it arrives."

Armond took a minute to look up the ship's location. "That won't be for another twelve hours. I'll have the captain contact you when the shuttle lands planet-side."

"Sounds good. Given the lack of security on the coms, we won't contact you unless it's an emergency. Use your judgment. We need to get Anantha to the PR's palace and stop Mortog."

"Understood."

Armond sent them back to Dani's focal point, and she pocketed the device. They found Father Arlo locking up the main entrance to the church.

"There you are. Is everything all right?"

"We don't know," Ian said. "We've been unable to reach my father since yesterday afternoon."

"That is troubling. May the Mother Goddess watch after him."

"Thank you."

Dani slipped her hand into his as they waited for the priest.

He sighed heavily as he dropped the keys into the bag he had slung over his shoulder. He'd posted a sign stating that the church was closed indefinitely. They were heading toward the cruiser that Darl Karton loaned them when the sound of footsteps echoed from behind. Someone was running up the path to the church. Ian stepped in front of the priest and pulled his weapon, Dani following suit.

A teen rounded the corner and stopped when he saw them.

Arlo pushed through. "Connor?"

"It's me, father."

"Put your weapons away."

The boy rushed to Arlo and wrapped his arms around him. "We need to go. They're coming for you."

They didn't need to hear any more. They rushed to the cruiser.

"Get in back and stay down," Dani told the priest and the boy.

"Where are we going?" Ian asked once they were off the ground.

"Get in the traffic pattern for Starfall," Arlo said. "It's about halfway." Once they were out of the city, Arlo climbed into the seat and gave a sigh of relief. "I'm too old to be sitting on the floor like that."

"Sorry," Dani said.

"No worries, my dear."

The boy didn't move from his spot on the floor. He just stared at the back of the seats.

Once they reached the designated intersection, Ian took them down, and they drove a quarter mile into the woods and parked near a black utility vehicle. The priest got out and spoke to the driver. A moment later the back swung open and a large, dark-skinned man stepped out. Arlo motioned for them to come over.

With a vacant look, the teen remained on the floor in the back. Probably in shock.

They approached the large man who extended his hand. "Father Arlo here tells me he's enlisted the help of the Cavacent clan. I'm Warder Zar."

Ian shook hands and introduced himself and Dani. "That's correct. Although at the moment, we may need your assistance."

"What is it?"

"My father is missing."

"Gods," Warder said. "Come, get in. We'll talk while we drive. Nocher," he bellowed, "take the cruiser with the boy to the transport hub and drop it there. I'll send a team to bring you both in."

A thin man jumped out and loped over to the cruiser.

Dani climbed in first, and then she and Ian helped Arlo step into the van with his bag. The van was well-lit inside, but there were no windows.

"Tell me what you know," Warder said to Ian as the vehicle lifted off.

"He was supposed to meet with Mortog yesterday afternoon. I wasn't concerned until today. I left him a message last night and another about an hour ago."

"Did you check with Mortog's office?"

Ian cleared his throat. "Not exactly. The thing is, we don't officially arrive on planet for another ten hours or so."

Warder frowned. "How's that?"

"Our transport ship hasn't arrived yet," Dani said.

Ian nodded. "We're not here."

"Well. As hallucinations go, you're pretty solid." Warder chuckled. "Before we go any farther, let's swap contact info, then I'll need you to shut down your coms. Make any calls you need to now. The underground is silent. No signals in or out except through me, and that's only if the planet is about to be invaded. It hasn't happened yet."

"I expected as much," Ian said. He and Dani turned off their units.

Warder nodded when they were done. "We have sensors underground. If your coms activate, our security will shoot you before asking for an explanation."

"Understood," Ian said.

Warder pulled out a com and started speaking. "Check Papa's house. See if he had a guest yesterday. Medium height. Graying hair. 'Bout my age. We're on our way to the beach." He disconnected and put the com into a steel box affixed to the floor of the van. He sealed the door with his psi. A readout indicated a fifteen-second countdown. When it finished, the door swung open, and a neat pile of ash sat where the com had been.

"You must go through a lot of coms," Dani said.

"That we do."

* * * *

Balastar approached the Cavacent Earth station with mixed emotions. He'd been sure Earth was going to be his new home, and although it was his base, he now felt more attached to his ship than anything else. He adjusted their approach and locked onto the docking beacon. He'd chosen well with this ship. Although more than he originally planned to spend, the extra comforts and upgrades made all the difference. The galley was off a large dining area, and the addition of a separate space for relaxing with a large view port added to the comfort. Not as posh as Rucon's ships, but perfectly adequate. He'd managed to leave Florin 5 a full day early by giving a discount to a client in order for them to get the goods to him faster.

Marco sat to his right with Mordo and Durgan standing behind them, taking in the view.

"She's a beautiful planet," Mordo said. "Though I'll probably always miss the purple hues of Sandaria."

"Indeed." Durgan placed a hand on Mordo's shoulder. "I'm most excited to see if Armond is able to use this device, as well."

Balastar's com signaled a call. He connected with psi and greeted Armond. "We're docking at the station now. We should be there in twenty minutes. Durgan can't wait for you to take a look at the second device."

"Nor can I. However, we have a situation. Do not delay. Come directly to Ria's villa. Mara is waiting with me here."

"On our way." Balastar relayed the message to the others.

The Cavacents' fully cloaked base station was impressive. It could accommodate five transport ships at one time. Balastar's instrumentation picked up the acceptance signal for bay three and he guided her in. Mordo, Durgan, and Marco grabbed their bags, and the four headed to the portal on the station. Three minutes later, they stepped through to Ria's villa.

Armond and Mara were waiting for them. Ian's mother looked like a child next to Armond.

"What's going on?" Marco asked.

Armond crossed his arms. "The situation on Mitah has become unstable. I've been told the chancellor is preparing to murder a large number of Curzans. Many of whom have psi. As you know, that makes the entire planetary rulership null and void. Ria contacted Ian. She's safe for now, but time is short. And Rucon has been missing since yesterday."

"That fell apart fast," Balastar said.

"I've just spoken to Anantha," Mara said. "He's agreed to redirect the nearest resources to Mitah, but it will take more than five hours. He, however, is only two hours from Earth. He's coming here with a small force. They will take the portal to Mitah as soon as possible with the intent to arrest Chancellor Mortog."

Durgan frowned. "Why does he not simply go to the nearest planet and have a portal created directly to Mitah? He's the Supreme Commander of the GTO for Goddess sake."

"I asked the same question," Mara said. "It appears that you and your fellow Portal Masters escaped the guild just in time. Portals are shutting down across the galaxy, and the new leader of the guild, Loc Zorton, is not responding to Anantha. He feels all interstellar portals should be considered suspect. Except ours, of course."

"Extraordinary," Mordo said. "Five-hundred years of stability in the guild gone in the blink of an eye." He turned to Armond. "All right, let's go find my brother."

Mara stepped forward.

Armond shook his head. "You are currently the only Cavacent descendant on Earth."

"You must think of all the people depending on us," Mara said.

Mordo's shoulders slumped as he nodded his agreement.

"I'm coming." Balastar stood next to Marco. "I pledged my fealty to Rucon."

"As you wish," Armond said. "I suggest we return to Mitah and wait. We'll want to maximize the number of people that can transport with the Commander." Portals had their limits. Four transports per hour with a maximum of eight-hundred pounds.

"Be careful," Mara said, "and find my husband."

* * * *

Mordo turned away from the portal. He understood the need for him to stay behind, but his instinct was to do something. "Durgan, perhaps there is yet something we can do to assist."

"What do you have in mind?"

"Let's start with mapping out the portals that are being shut down. There must be a reason for it. Perhaps they are isolating an area of the galaxy?"

Durgan agreed, and the two took the subterranean tunnel to their smaller but more opulent villa above Lago Como.

After an hour of mapping out the failing portals, Mordo poured another cup of tea for himself and Durgan. "There doesn't appear to be any pattern to what they're shutting down."

Durgan stood and paced by the windows of their study. "What if they aren't doing it?"

"Why else would they fail? Never have I heard of portals shutting down on their own."

"Nor I, but what if…" Durgan spun around and pulled up a holo screen that took up the entire back wall. "Com, run a list of all Portal Masters involved in the creation of the portals on this display." They waited a moment for the list to compile. "Now, highlight in red the following." Durgan stated the names of the nine Portal Masters that accompanied them to Earth.

"Great Goddess, you've done it." Mordo said.

Under each failed portal anywhere from three to all nine of the Portal Masters' names were lit up in red.

Durgan nodded, brows furrowed. "Let's think about this. What does it mean?"

"For starters, it means this is why the guild was restricted to the compound on Sandaria." Mordo stood as well. Excitement coursed through him.

"Yes," Durgan said. "What if the feed to the portals goes away when we do?" He stopped. "This implies some static device is being fed. We had no idea it worked that way."

"We didn't," Mordo said, "but I'd be willing to bet the Masters' Council does."

The two smiled and clasped each other.

Mordo squeezed Durgan's arm. "This is extraordinary. This is why it was always treated as a sacred service. Why Portal Masters weren't allowed family and swore their lives to the guild."

Durgan rubbed his chin and nodded. "Given a choice between loyalty to the guild and that of family, many would eventually choose family. Wives and children, especially." He turned to face Mordo. "How much of what we thought we knew of the guild is even real? What of the God we've been worshiping?"

"There is a deep mystery here, my friend. Given what we now know of the alternate psi portal devices, it would possibly imply there is something similar being kept on Sandaria."

"Something immobile perhaps," Durgan agreed. "Gods, but I would like to get my hands on that." His eyes shone bright at the thought.

"So their portals are going to continue to fail." Mordo couldn't hold still. "It takes time to find and train new masters. They must be panicked."

"Desperate."

"Yes. I'll call Mara. Supreme Commander Anantha needs to have this information." Mordo smiled again. "Can you imagine the look on Zorton's face right now?"

"It is an image I will not soon forget, my friend."

Chapter 15

Ty found the security measures Warder Zar employed for getting everyone returned to the underground base impressive. Their escape from jail in a tagless cruiser had been a risk. If security had detected a vehicle without an ID, they would have known something was up. Today, they used a utility van that broadcast a tag from a bogus corporation. It wasn't until they neared the underground entrance that they stopped broadcasting, and that was only when surveillance around the area declared it free of any Mitah security vehicles. Getting to the entrance itself was another three-phase process.

Heavy clouds gathered over the mountain peaks. A storm was coming. It was just as well they were going underground. Once inside the old tunnels, a low-range frequency triggered the lights that immediately switched off as they passed.

Ria's psi rippled through Ty. *"They better give us our own room."* She smiled at him, and as always, he was struck at how amazing it was to have found her. She was perfect, and she was his.

"In need of a little sleep, are you, Red?"

"Yeah, sleep. That's what I want."

Her psi pulsed, and his body responded in kind. *"You better stop that, or I'll take you right here and now."*

She grinned and pulled away.

Ty glanced out the only window in the back of the cruiser at the dark tunnel behind them. He and Ria should be holed up in a cabin someplace enjoying their new bond. Instead, they were fighting for not only their lives, but many others, as well.

They finally made it to the main chamber, and the cruiser parked in the designated area. The sheer size of the place still amazed him. They climbed out, and a small, wiry woman, who didn't look much older than Olivia, approached.

"Welcome back." She and Olivia exchanged hugs.

Olivia turned to the others. "This is Minnar. She's in charge when my father and I are gone."

The others said their hellos. "I take it he's out?" Olivia asked.

"Yeah. Left in a rush. Not sure when to expect him. I hear you have some good news."

Olivia nodded. "Wonderboy here decoded the texts." She smiled at Ty.

He felt Ria's pride and was glad the two women seemed to have patched things up. "You can thank Bella. She figured out what I was doing wrong."

"That's great news." Minnar's happiness was guarded. They all knew time was short. "Come, I've set up the conference room with a recorder."

"Aren't you worried about the signal?" Merek asked.

Minnar shook her head. "Room's shielded."

They made their way to the conference room where they'd met Warder the first day. Thick drapes now covered the windows that looked out over the open space below. A large screen hung from one wall. They all filed in and sat down to plan their vid.

Merek, Trin, and Bella simply watched.

"We need to keep it as simple as possible," Olivia said.

"And short," Ty added. "We don't want to get cut off before we finish our message."

They sorted through the pages of the journal and selected the one with the most obvious text source. In the end, they decided that Ty and Ria both would present the information with Ria finishing the address with a call to the GTO.

Ty started with, "Attention all inhabitants of planet Mitah. We have proof that a segment of native Curzans had psi when the planetary rulership was awarded. Under the old empire, that would mean the Rulership was, and has always been, invalid."

Ria went next. "I am not from this planet. I am an Earth Protector under the clan of Lord Rucon Cavacent. I have witnessed the injustice first hand. We are asking the GTO to help us end the genocide being systematically carried out by Chancellor Mortog. Everyone on this planet should have rights and the freedom to live and learn as they wish."

Ty finished up as the vid zoomed in on the text and key. "We present the following images as proof of our claims. And we are warning all natives to move with caution until we can gain our rightful status on Mitah."

"That's it," Minnar said after the still of the text and key ran another sixty seconds. I've got runners ready to deliver copies to our people at the networks. They've been instructed to set the vid to loop and get out as soon as possible. Let's hope this works."

"It will," Ria said.

Ty cast her a look. He loved her optimism and wished he shared it.

* * * *

Ria stood leaning against the window frame wishing there was more she could do. Below, a large cruiser pulled in and parked by the main tunnel. Warder Zar stepped out, followed by an older man and two others. "Ty, look! It's Dani and Ian. Come on." She bolted out the door and down the stairs. Crossing the open space, she collided with Dani in a massive hug. "What are you doing here?" Ria said.

"I could ask you the same," Dani replied. "Is this where you've been hiding out?"

"Not exactly. We just got back about an hour ago."

Ian stepped in for a quick hug, as well. "Good to see you, Ria."

"Thanks, boss. You too." A wave of Ty's jealousy rippled over her. She laughed and turned to introduce him. "Come here, Ty. I want to introduce you to my boss and my bestie."

Ty approached looking guarded but reached out to shake Ian's hand. "Ty Sordina. Nice to meet you properly."

"Agreed," Ian said. "Better than the previous circumstances."

Ria threw Ian a glare. He didn't need to bring that up.

"We have a lot to discuss." Ian clasped Ty on the shoulder, diffusing the tension.

"That we do." Warder's voice echoed in the large space. "I suggest we retire to the conference room. Have you made the vid?"

"Just finished," Olivia said. "Come on, we'll let you check it out before we send the runners."

Arlo gave Ty a quick embrace, and they followed Warder and Olivia.

Dani fell in step next to Ria as the rest headed back to the shielded room. "So?"

"So?" Ria said, trying not to blush.

Dani nudged her with psi and nodded in Ty's direction. "Is he your psi-mate?"

Ria nodded.

Dani squealed.

"Shh. You're acting like a teenager."

Dani gave her shoulders a squeeze. "I'm just so happy for you."

"Thanks. It's pretty amazing. Now we just have to get out of this mess alive."

Back in the room, Arlo greeted everyone, and they waited while the others watched the vid.

"Send it out," Warder said. "Make sure they coordinate broadcasts and mail it to as many people as you can. Don't stay in any one location and go silent as soon as you're done."

"Will do." Minnar left to deliver the vid to their sources.

"This is quite an operation you have here," Ian said.

"Over twenty-five years in the making," Warder said. "But it's time we leave this place and live in peace on our own planet."

"There's only one way to do that." Olivia crossed her arms and leaned on the table. "Mortog has to go."

"Are you absolutely sure about the texts?" Dani asked.

"It's not one hundred percent," Ty said. "That will take time. But I'm sure enough. We have the essence right. We already know some Curzans have psi. The texts just give us proof of the initial cover-up."

"Then we need to arrest Mortog," Ian said.

Olivia scowled. "You can't touch him. Not on this planet."

"Maybe we can't," Ian said, "but Supreme Commander Torril Anantha and his forces can. With any luck, he should have received word by now and is en route."

"When will they get here?" Ty asked.

"I won't know until we get back outside and I can contact my people."

Olivia slammed her fist on the table. "He's getting ready to kill a large number of Watersedge Curzans now. We don't have time for your GTO. What we do have"—she pulled out a sheet of paper—"is Mortog's schedule. I've isolated a vulnerable window just a few hours from now."

Ria was about to speak when a tall thin man and a teen entered the room.

"Thank the Goddess, you're alive," Ria said, recognizing the boy from the marketplace.

Everyone looked at her. "Him." She indicated the teen. "I was worried about what happened to him."

The boy backed up, his body tense.

Ria held up her hands. "It's okay. We're on your side."

"You must have me confused with someone else." The teen looked terrified.

"No," Dani said, taking a closer look at him. "I didn't recognize him before. It was dark. You're the one Jara had arrested when we were here the first trip."

Ty came over and stood next to Ria. "What are you two talking about?"

"Our first trip here," Ria said. "The day we met. Jara had him arrested. I tried to find out what happened to him when we returned to Mitah for the ball, but the local police said they had no record of any teens taken into custody that day. I was afraid they might have...well, you know."

Ty tilted his head. "That doesn't make sense. I saw him later that day."

"That's not possible," Ria said. "Jara had him hauled off."

Ty looked to the teen. "Connor? What's she talking about."

"I don't know," he said. "Like I said, they must have me confused with someone else." He shifted his weight from foot to foot.

"He's lying," Ria said to Ty. *"It's him. I know it is. Jara had him."* She sensed Ty's conclusion as his anger washed over her. Traitor.

Ty stepped forward, grabbed Connor by the shirt, and slammed him against the wall next to the door. "Why'd he let you go, Connor? They never let us go. They kill us."

"I didn't do anything," Connor whined.

Ty slammed him into the wall again. "Fracking liar. You're killing your own people."

"And you're killing my sister," Connor yelled back. "You keep telling me to wait. That you'll bring her to Watersedge, but you never do. She's going to be thirteen next year. They'll sell her. If we lose track of her, we may never find her again."

Chaos broke out as Ty slammed the teen into the wall again. "I told you she's on our schedule. That we would get her once we had the others that need our help first." Ty's hand was around Connor's throat.

"Ty, stop!" Ria stepped back, shocked at the extreme hatred rolling off her psi-mate. It affected her, felt like her own. She couldn't move. The memory of Ty's parents' death played in her mind, and she was sure it was all he could see as well.

Merek grabbed hold of Ty and pulled him off as Warder and the thin man stepped in and kept Connor from bolting out the door.

"You killed Jafferies," Ty said, struggling to free himself from Merek's grip.

"Jafferies was dying anyway," Connor said, face pale.

Ty roared out in frustration. "And what about the others? Were they dying anyway?"

Connor looked like he was going to puke. "I didn't have any choice. I had to give them names. Jara busted me a few months ago." He started crying. "They were going to kill me."

"He's just a boy, Ty." Ria was shaking now.

Merek let him go, and Ty turned to Ria and wrapped her in his arms. *"Gods, I' m sorry."* He stroked her hair. *"Betrayal makes me insane."*

"Come on. We need to get out of here. Let Warder take care of this." She turned to Warder. "We're going for a walk."

"Good idea. Go out the back there." He pointed to a tunnel on the far side from where they'd entered. "That goes for about a mile and is covered by repellers. Don't go past the opening."

* * * *

Mortog sat across from the president of Sandaria, Gordat Prayda. Where once the title would have implied an entire empire, now it encompassed a single planet. It was a rather important planet, however, as it was home to the Portal Masters' guild.

Prayda was a fleshy man with rheumy eyes. He'd had the Portal Masters create a portal inside Mortog's personal detention center. It seemed an obvious choice since he doubted the president would want to be seen. Once Prayda had verified the man Mortog had detained was in fact Rucon Cavacent, he joined Mortog in his office.

"Are you sure you have everything under control?" Prayda asked.

"Quite. I've placed a mole in the Watersedge Underground. In fact, I believe enough time has passed. Let's find out where they are, shall we?"

"I assume you placed a tracker on the man, but won't they scan him? Surely, they're not that backward."

"Sadly, no. My healers implanted a bio-marker." Mortog enjoyed the man's look of puzzlement.

"I have quite the remarkable research team here. Two years ago my people created psi-bands. Wonderfully handy devices that restrict a person's psi to their own bodies. You wear them like handcuffs and are rendered powerless."

The president leaned forward. "That is extraordinary. I must have these psi-bands."

"Of course. I will see that you get a supply. Now, my team recently surprised me with another lovely device. It's a biological marker. Completely untraceable until it's activated, at which point it becomes a tracking device. It's not very long-lived at this time, but they tell me they're working on it."

"Excellent." Gordat rubbed his hands together. "This promises to be a beneficial relationship, indeed. Let's see where your man is."

"More like a boy, but let's. It's time we find out where the rats are hiding." Gordat brought up a holo screen with the map of the Watersedge area and activated the marker. The image panned out and refocused on an area outside of Starfall.

"No. That can't be." He called his lead of development and explained the situation.

"I'm quite sure it's accurate. You're mole is not in Watersedge but near Starfall. Is that all?"

Mortog didn't bother replying. He disconnected and keyed in another number.

Prayda snickered. "Looks like your underground is a little closer to home than you thought."

"Sou, get in here," Mortog yelled into his com.

The lieutenant entered the room along with two guards. "What is it?"

"This." Mortog blew up the image. "Our mole is just outside Starfall."

Sou inspected the screen, then pulled up an image of his own. The spot was overgrown with trees and foliage. "There's nothing there." He entered a few more commands and a rapid series of images flashed by, superimposed on the terrain. The image froze. "But there was. It was an ancient transportation hub. The barbarians used to ride in long carriages that traveled on steel rails underground."

"So what you're saying," Prayda said, "is that your underground is underground?"

Mortog wanted to slap the man, but knew better. He was a much-needed ally. Although the relative importance of Sandaria itself was now in question, there was no doubt of the power of the Portal Masters that resided there.

"I'm quite sure Watersedge is full of Curzans masquerading as Mitans. Jara's intelligence was sound. No matter. We'll take care of this nest first."

Sou's image zoomed in a little to the left of the signal. "There is a small farming village here. I'll send out a team and check it out."

"Find the entrances to that space," Mortog said. "Now."

"Yes, sir."

"Why bother?" Prayda asked.

"Excuse me?" Mortog raised an eyebrow.

"Why bother finding the entrances? If it were me, I'd simply destroy the place. A few well-placed bombs and your problem is neatly buried."

Mortog burst out laughing. "I do believe we are of the same mind. That is an excellent idea. Sou, see to it. But find and monitor the entrances just in case. I don't want any survivors."

"Yes, sir," Sou said. He turned to go but froze in the doorway, staring at his com.

"What is it?" Mortog asked.

Sou's face went nearly white.

"What is it?" Mortog barked.

Sou instructed his com to project a vid feed. The bottom corner identified it as a local news station.

Mortog clenched his teeth as he watched the *crag* Ty Sordina and Rucon's female EP. He remained silent as the pair talked of crimes against the Curzans and showed some bogus texts. Incredulously, the feed repeated itself after a brief pause. Mortog's anger increased with each second.

The visiting president, Gordat Prayda, stood. "I believe you have some damage control to do. I will leave you to it and take care of my own house cleaning. After I finish with Rucon, I will be returning to Sandaria. You'll want to send someone to dispose of the body. Contact me when you're done here, and we'll continue our discussions."

He left the office without another word.

Mortog swung on Sou. "What are you waiting for? I want them all dead, and pull those feeds. Now."

* * * *

Dani sighed. Connor was just a teen, but he was responsible for the deaths of many Curzans.

Warder waited until Ty and Ria were gone before speaking to the man who'd brought Connor in. "You scanned him?"

"Of course."

He turned to Connor and stared a moment. "This is a sad day."

"Indeed," Father Arlo agreed. "At least we know who our mole is. Watching Connor got me to thinking."

"What about?" Merek asked.

"The texts seem to indicate that from the beginning there were those with and without psi on our world." Arlo rubbed his neck.

"Go on," Olivia said.

"That type of friction, envy from those without psi, could explain why our ancestors nearly destroyed this planet. Having those with and without psi lends itself to a natural class divide."

Warder scratched his days old stubble. "It's certainly possible."

"Maybe that's how they got away with the planetary rulership," Olivia said. "They could prove the natives had no psi. As long as they selected the right Curzans."

"Things are going to get interesting here pretty soon. In the meantime, we need to decide what to do with him." Warder's anger was obvious.

"Don't hurt him," Trin said. She'd watched the whole thing silently with an arm wrapped around the young teen, Bella. "He's so young."

"We should kill him for what he's done. You understand that?" Warder said. Connor paled.

"No," both Trin and Bella cried out.

"Not on our watch," Dani said to Ian.

"Let's wait and see how this plays out."

"What he did is horrid," Bella said, "but he was afraid for his life and trying to help his sister. You know what Gordat's people are like. If they had him for any length of time, he wouldn't have been...treated well." Bella was near tears.

"Killing him is not what the Mother Goddess would want, I'm quite sure," Father Arlo said.

"It is not what I want either." Warder looked tired.

Dani was about to make a suggestion when a man dressed in Mortog's security outfit burst into the room. She and Ian drew their lasers and aimed.

"Halt," Warder said calmly. "He's one of ours."

The man was breathing heavily. "We must evacuate immediately."

"What has happened?" Warder asked.

"Mortog found us. He's planning to bomb the underground. We must hurry. As the newest member of Sou's security team my absence is going to be noticed."

"How could he find us?"

"He bugged the boy. I came as soon as I could." The man nodded toward Connor.

Warder turned to the man who accompanied Connor. "Nocher?"

"I scanned him personally."

"Scan him again."

Nocher withdrew a device and powered it on. Within a few seconds, it glowed red. "He was clean! I swear, I scanned him."

"Execute evacuation procedures," Warder said. "Nocher, you're in charge of the boy. The rest of you, follow me."

An alarm sounded, and below people ran toward the perimeter of the underground.

"Wait," Dani said. "We have to get Ria and Ty."

Warder shook his head with a saddened look. "No time. The tunnel they're in won't accommodate our cruisers. They'll have to make it out on their own. I'm sorry. My people come first."

"We can't just leave them," Dani said.

"You come with us or go after them on foot," Warder said. "I'm sorry, but I can't jeopardize the lives of my fellow Curzans."

"Understood," Ian said. "No more than we can leave our people behind. Go." He and Warder nodded to each other. He took hold of Dani's hand and headed out the door. *"We'll catch up to them and have Armond port us out."*

Dani smacked her forehead. *"Shit. Why didn't we give them a focal point?"*

"I'm still not used to having these things. Didn't even occur to me until after they were gone."

* * * *

Anger slid away, and the adrenaline rush left Ria rattled as they walked down the cold, damp tunnel. She inhaled deeply and let it out before speaking. "We need to talk about what happened back there."

Ty squeezed her hand. "I know. I'm sorry, but I honestly can't control my anger sometimes."

"I figured that out," Ria said. "The problem is, it affects me, too. I went a little crazy. I was shaking. I really need you to not do that anymore."

Ty stopped and turned her to him. He pulled her tight and his psi wrapped around and through her own. "I'm sorry, Red. I'll do my best. There's just so much anger. I see my parents and…" He bowed his head.

"It's okay. I'm here." She squeezed back. She knew his pain and understood how he lost control. "Look at me." Pushing back enough, she placed her hand on his face. "Between the two of us, we'll learn how to tame that anger. We'll turn it into something else." She tilted forward on her toes and kissed him deeply.

The sound of running feet had them spinning apart and pressing against the side of the tunnel.

"Ria, Ty!" It was Dani's voice, still out of sight around a bend in the tunnel.

"What is it? What's wrong?" Ria called back.

"Come here. We have to go. The underground's cover has been blown. Get over here, we can port out."

They bolted off the wall, but halted at the sound of an explosion. Dust billowed down the tunnel as another explosion rocked the walls.

"Come on, we have to get to the entrance." Ty spun her around and they ran. Psi gave them the needed boost in speed as they outpaced the dust behind them. Barely. A few moments later, they came out into a dense undergrowth. Rain pelted from above and soaked them within seconds. They moved to the side as a blast of air and dust burst from the tunnel.

"There are no repellers out here," Ria said.

"The rain should help mask our smell and our sounds." Ty looked around and fixated on a cliff face in the distance.

Ria followed his gaze and fear stabbed her heart. *"That's where we were running to in the dream."*

Ty didn't answer as a voice bellowed from someplace overhead. "Halt. Remain where you are. I repeat, remain where you are and do not move."

"Like hell." Ria pulled at Ty's shirt, and they took off. Deeper and deeper into the forest they fled. Branches scraped bloody gashes into Ria's arms and legs. A branch whipped back from Ty's passing and nearly snapped into her eye. *"Watch it with the branches."*

"Sorry, Red." He shot her a troubled glance. *"There's a reason we were going for the cliff face."*

The memory of the dream superimposed itself on reality.

Ria ducked under a large limb and tried to shake off the dream. *"And?"*

"There's a weapons cache in those cliffs. It's our only hope. If your boss is right, all we have to do is stay alive long enough for the GTO commander to come and take over."

"Yeah, but I'm pretty sure we know how this ends."

Ty slowed to a stop, breathing heavy. *"We won't let it end that way."*

Much as she wanted to believe him, she'd lived that dream too many times. She looked into his gray eyes. Gods, she loved this man. She stood a little taller and shifted into battle mode. Mentally shoving her fear to the background, she nodded.

Somewhere down the hill and to their left, the scream of a worick split the night.

"It may just be responding to the cruiser," Ty said. *"Less than a mile. Come on. We can make it."*

Ria followed her psi-mate and sent a little prayer to the Mother Goddess to see them through this.

Chapter 16

Rucon Cavacent was not a happy man. Chancellor Mortog would pay for this folly. His wrists were chafed from struggle, but he had to admit the bands were impressive. Never had he heard of such a thing. It was obvious they somehow contained one's psi to the range of the physical body. Although not painful, the sensation was uncomfortable and foreign, to say the least. As well as the bands, he was restrained by straps that held him to a steel table at a nearly vertical angle. The room was sparsely furnished. Nothing but a table and a few chairs. Bright lights faced him. In the floor below him was a drain. There was only one reason for a room such as this. He was contemplating how to escape when the door opened. It wasn't Mortog who entered, however, but Gordat Prayda.

Rucon's anger surged. Because of the bands, his psi had no way to expend the increased energy. Now, the restraints became painful. He would have to be cautious of his emotions. "You filthy excuse for a soul. I should have known you had a hand in this."

Gordat closed the door behind him and sauntered over to Rucon. "Such foul words from someone in your, shall we say, compromised position." He slapped Rucon in the face, which caused him to laugh.

"You hit like a child."

Gordat spun around and retrieved a nasty-looking metal rod from a rack on the wall. "Perhaps this will have a greater effect. You didn't think I was just going to let you go, did you?" He swung the rod back and slammed it into Rucon's left knee.

Combined with the pulse of his restrained psi, the pain surged through his body, tipping him into blackness. The shock of ice-cold water over his head had him coughing and trying to focus.

"No, no. You must stay awake for this. It wouldn't do to have you miss out on all the fun. I've waited a very long time for this day, Rucon. Looks like we'll need to experiment a little to see how best to extract my revenge and keep you around to enjoy it."

* * * *

Mortog paced in front of his office windows. A storm raged outside. The sky was dark and wind whipped rain against the glass. *Good. This weather should help mask our little extermination.*

Sou had detonated the explosives a few minutes earlier. The news stations had stopped spewing that incessant feed of lies, and investigations were underway to determine how it had happened. Mortog closed his eyes and imagined Curzans dying en mass, like rats on a sinking ship, and smiled. He snapped back to attention. "Do you have the exits covered?"

"They're covered, but this rain isn't going to help any."

Five minutes later Sou's voice interrupted his thoughts. "I'm missing a team that was stationed on the west entrance, but we have a hit at the northern exit. Two people on foot. Hold on." Sou spoke to someone else a moment, then returned. "It's them. That Sordina boy and the redhead."

Anger rippled over him. "Send me the coordinates. Do not lose them. Do not kill them. I'm going to end this personally." He turned to go to his cruiser. "And find out what happened to your missing team."

* * * *

Dani's hands covered her face. The comfort of Ian's arms surrounding her meant they'd made it out of the tunnel. She opened her eyes to find Armond looking at them with a raised eyebrow.

"Thanks," she said as Ian let her go and proceeded to dust her off. A layer of fine dust from the blast covered them from head to toe. "That was close."

"Too close," Ian said.

"I hope they made it out."

Armond studied his com. "Would you care to explain how is it I ported you from approximately twenty-five feet underground?"

"Turns out the Starfall Underground was underground," Ian said.

"Mortog bombed it, the bastard. Warder and his people should have made it out, but there were children in that group." Dani couldn't believe the chancellor would go to such lengths. "That man needs to be stopped. His rights are forfeit. I'll kill him myself."

"Easy," Ian said.

It was then she noticed Balastar and Marco. "Hey guys, good to see you." Marco was an EP, but Balastar was here on his own free will. "Thanks for coming, Balastar."

He gave her a nod and a wink.

"I just spoke with your mother, Ian," Armond said. "Supreme Commander Anantha should be here soon. It's been an hour since Balastar and I returned. We have four ports available."

"All right," Ian said. "In the meantime, find the old maps of the planets subterranean rail. We need to figure out where Ria and Ty are going to come out and get someone there as soon as possible."

Ian's com buzzed, and he glanced down. "It's Warder." He connected. "Did everyone make it out?" There was a brief pause. "Glad to hear it. Can you send someone to where Ria and Ty will exit? They'll need help." Ian nodded affirmative. "Thank you. As soon as Commander Anantha arrives, we'll head to the palace. We'll apprehend Mortog and find my father. Stay in touch."

Ian slipped the com back into his pocket. "They ran into Mortog's security but overpowered them. He's dropping off some people, then he'll take a team to help Ty and Ria. Armond, I need you to stay here. If anyone needs rescue, you'll be ready. As soon as the Commander arrives, we'll go straight to the palace. Once he's established his control, we'll arrange a planet-wide broadcast on all stations notifying the citizens that the GTO is now in command. Did he say when his main forces would arrive?"

"He did not. I would prefer to accompany you. You may meet with resistance."

"We'll almost certainly meet with resistance, but you are our backup. You need to stay put."

"Yes, sir."

Dani glanced at Armond. "I know it's not easy staying here, but Ian and I are proof that your being able to port us out at a moment's notice is the most important thing you can be doing."

"I understand this," Armond said. "But you are correct, it is not easy."

"One thing's for sure," Ian said. "As soon as we see Ria, she gets a focal point."

Less than five minutes later the Supreme Commander, Torril Anantha, and three of his security walked out of the portal. Another thirteen, uniformed officers, men and women, came through in quick succession.

The commander was a large man, a few years younger than Rucon. Lean and fit, he exuded confidence.

Ian made the introductions.

"Any word of your father?" Torril asked.

"None." Ian shook his head. "But we feel he is most likely being held at the planetary ruler's Palace. Chancellor Mortog has been residing there and effectively in charge for the past seven years."

Dani stepped forward. "You're just in time. Mortog bombed the Starfall Underground headquarters."

"Casualties?"

"None that we know of," Ian said. "But one of my own and her Curzan psi-mate were separated from us. Warder Zar, the leader of the resistance is going to look for them now."

"Good. Let's go find your father and take down this corrupt regime."

They summoned a private transport cruiser in order to avoid detection for as long as possible. Anantha's team contained powerful psi, and between them, they were heavily shielded. They followed the traffic flow around the palace. Even through the pelting rain, it was an opulent building of bright white and gold trim. A bit over the top for Dani's tastes.

The cruiser set down at the visitor's entrance and they made their way inside. Such a large group including uniformed soldiers garnered the attention of security before they were five steps in. Three men in dark suits flanked by four guards approached them. Two of the suited men were tall and lanky but the middle one was short and pudgy. Pudge appeared to be the one in command. The guards and the soldiers squared off, weapons drawn on both sides. More guards were being summoned by the woman behind a reception desk.

"What's the meaning of this?" Pudge asked.

"Everyone just relax," Anantha said. "I'm Supreme Commander of the newly restructured Sandarian military and joint commander of the Galactic Trade Organization."

Pudge looked like he was about to argue but Torril cut him off. "I have a full battalion en route as we speak. Since Mitah has been under a planetary rulership sanctioned by the Sandarian Empire for the past one hundred and seventy-eight years, I suggest you accept our authority and put away your weapons."

"He's right, you know." A bald man carrying an arm full of papers rushed toward them. "Unless you and Mortog's men are planning on taking on the entire Sandarian military?"

Pudge's face reddened. "Of course not. I assume you have identification?"

"Are you daft, man?" The bald dude asked.

Dani was starting to like this guy.

"Have you not seen his image plastered over every interplanetary feed we receive?"

The guards looked increasingly uncomfortable. The two tall, suited guys seemed to simultaneously decide to throw Pudge under the bus and both acknowledged Anantha's authority. The guards lowered their weapons and Pudge acted as though the whole thing was his idea.

"Excellent," Anantha said. "We are here to relieve Chancellor Mortog of his duties. Take us to him."

"If you will pardon the interruption," the bald man said. "I am Terrance Florensham, chief administrative assistant to Chancellor Mortog. The chancellor is not here right now. However, it is most urgent that you come with me. Lord Cavacent is being detained on Mortog's orders. I fear for his well being."

"Show us the way," Ian said.

Terrance led them down a corridor on the backside of Mortog's office. "I believe Mortog can access this area from his office, but only he knows how." He was surprisingly quick as he made his way to the end of the hall, stopping just short of the back wall. Glancing around them, he addressed the commander in a hushed voice. "The newly elected president of Sandaria was here earlier. They set up a portal in this little room from hell. I believe he had a special interest in Lord Cavacent."

Ian's anger rolled over Dani, colliding with her own.

"Let us in, now," Ian said.

"Please, be careful." He raised his hand on the left side of the hall, and a panel slid open. The angle of the entry prevented them from seeing anything, but a muffled groan let them know the space wasn't empty.

"I don't sense your father at all," Dani said.

"That was his voice, I'm sure of it, but I don't sense him either."

Dani and Ian rushed down a short hall and into what could only be called a torture chamber. Gordat Prayda turned to them with a snarl on his face.

"This is not over," Prayda said before taking three steps to the side and disappearing. Sandarian Portal Masters might not be responding to the Supreme Commander, but they were helping Prayda.

Dani and Ian rushed to Rucon's side. Ian adjusted the table to lay flat and used his laser to cut Rucon free. Once he sliced the cords around his wrists, Rucon's psi trembled around them.

"Gods," Ian said. "What is that?" He fingered the bands.

"They're called psi-bands." Terrance approached from behind. "Mortog has a team of scientists who specialize in technology that can be particularly subversive. I shall not miss the chancellor."

"Do you have a healer at the palace?" Dani asked.

"I have already taken the liberty of summoning them. I'm afraid they are not unused to situations such as this. Just last week it was a mere slip of a boy...and it wasn't his first time."

"Connor," Ian said.

Dani gently brushed some hair out of Rucon's eyes. "Are you okay?"

Rucon licked his parched lips. "I will be. Fortunately Prayda likes to play with his food."

Two healers in white rushed in and started to work.

Anantha stood a few paces back, out of their way.

Rucon greeted the commander. "Prayda's actions were unprovoked."

Anantha nodded. "I will initiate a trade block with Sandaria. We have a situation with the Portal Masters there."

He explained about the failing portals across the galaxy. "It's only a theory at this point, but your brother is fairly confident."

The commander turned to Terrance. "Thank you for your excellent sense of priorities."

The man bowed. "I am most relieved at your intervention on our planet." Shame rolled off him, and Dani felt sorry for what his life must have been like.

"Do you know where Mortog went?"

"He did not say, but I believe it had something to do with the Curzans."

"He's after Ria and Ty. We need to find them," Dani said.

Ian turned to Anantha. "We're going after my EP."

The commander didn't need further explanation. "I will see to your father's safety. Go."

* * * *

"Commander Anantha." Loc sat in his office looking at the commander's vid feed. "My apologies for not returning your communiqués sooner. As you've undoubtedly noticed, the guild is having some problems of its own." Loc had ignored the calls and requests from Supreme Commander Anantha as long as he could. He couldn't afford to alienate the GTO further, so damage control was in order.

"Obviously, we have noticed." The commander did not look happy. "Would you care to explain why portals are failing?"

Loc straightened up in his chair. "I'm sure you are familiar with the nature of the guild. We do not share our religion with outsiders. I'm afraid this is something of a crisis. I assure you we are working on a resolution. We hope to have the portals reinstated as soon as possible. I should think less than a month." That might be pushing it but was what the commander wanted to hear.

"I would ask that you keep me informed on the progress."

"Of course, commander."

"There is one more thing."

Loc nodded and waited.

"President Gordat Prayda attempted to kill Lord Cavacent today. He has overstepped his authority. I have issued a warrant for his arrest. I assume this won't be a problem for you?"

Loc struggled to keep his face neutral. *That fool.* "I am sorry to hear that. Of course, your request will be honored. What would you like done with him?"

"Hold him. I will send a squad to pick him up for trial." The commander blew out a long breath, looking tired.

Loc imagined his job was probably one of the most trying in the universe right now, but somehow he failed to find sympathy. "As you wish. You will be notified when he is in custody. Is that all?"

"For now."

The link dropped and his holo disappeared. Loc stood. He would need security to apprehend the president. He wasn't going to enjoy what he had to do next, but he didn't regret it either. Gordat Prayda had been the perfect puppet president on Sandaria after the fall of the emperor, but his ego and greed were tiresome. Fortunately, the problem was about to resolve itself quite nicely. The man's greed had sealed his own fate.

* * * *

Rain pelted Ria's face as they scrambled over sharp boulders at the base of the cliff face. She'd been doing a good job of not thinking about the dream until her foot slipped and she crashed down on one knee. She muffled a cry and looked up to find Ty reaching down for her. She didn't state the obvious. They both remembered the exact moment this happened in the dream.

"Come on, Red. We're almost there."

Ria wiped rain from her eyes, but it was a futile effort. She followed behind Ty, feeling like a prisoner being led to her execution. The woricks had been trailing them for the last five minutes, their leathery bodies darting between the trees below. It forced them to the base of the cliffs in order to limit the possible direction of attack. They were soaked to the bone and the constant use of psi had them both drained. They had no weapons, but one thing was working for them—for some reason, the Mitah security team had backed off and was hovering a safe distance away.

"Are you sure they don't know about the weapons cache?" Ria asked.

"As sure as I can be."

They continued on. It was a game of cat and mouse. The team had the ability to kill them on the spot but was doing nothing more than track them.

"There," Ty said, breathing heavily.

Ahead, a tall vertical slit opened in the cliff face. Ria knew it reached to the top, knew the rain would be pouring in from above. She'd been to that party too many times. It didn't end well. "Ty, this is crazy." She glanced back to the hovering cruiser. "What are they doing? Why haven't they attacked us yet?"

The arrival of a second security cruiser answered her question. This one came straight for them. As if on cue, or maybe because they'd been spooked, four woricks launched an attack.

Ty pushed her behind him and backed them against the cliff face.

"Oh, you did not just do that. Move your ass over, Ty."

He wasn't happy but he moved.

The woricks bounded up the incline from the treeline. Ria grabbed a couple of hefty rocks and readied for the attack.

A flash of light caught her attention. The cruiser had engaged its weapons. That was it. One way or another, they were done.

Ty shot her a look. "I love you, Red."

There was no time to answer. The woricks were only feet away when the cruiser shot a laser cannon and blasted three of the animals. The charred carcasses hissed in the rain. The fourth animal hesitated a moment before launching itself at them. Ty shoved her sideways and the animal smashed into the cliff face, its left shoulder seared off from the laser cannon. It continued to wail with its last breath.

Ria landed hard on her ass, but Ty had kept his feet. He jumped the carcass and knelt by her side. "You okay?"

"Yeah."

He reached out and gave her a hand up.

"This is off-script from the dream, Ty. What's going on? Who is that?"

"I don't know, but we've already changed the outcome. We're going to make it."

The cruiser touched down as close to them as possible. Ria thought maybe Ty was right until Chancellor Mortog himself stepped out.

"Frack," Ty said trying to ease them closer to the crevice.

Mortog's face was red and his hair quickly became plastered to his head. He stomped toward them, robes billowing out, looking every bit the crazed madman. "Where do you think you're going?" he bellowed. He slipped and nearly fell before reaching them. He had a laser gun aimed at Ty's chest. "You cost me a good man and made my security forces look like imbeciles." The way the rain poured down his face was comical except for the insanity in his eyes.

"Ty." Ria grabbed his arm knowing there was nothing she could do.

"Your luck has run out. And your little whore is next." Mortog smiled and aimed.

Ria pushed Ty with everything she had. Pain shot through her left glute as she slammed into a boulder. The scene in front of her took on a surreal dimension as Mortog's head exploded in blood and gray matter.

"What the frack?" Ria sat upright, wincing with pain from her butt cheek.

Ty scrambled over to her and checked for injuries. She smiled at him and laughed. It came out sounding more than a little crazy.

Above them, Warder Zar was in a cruiser with three men, all with weapons aimed at the remaining security team. On the other side of the team were Dani and Ian in another vehicle, darts drawn, and in some bizarre twist, a third security vehicle, weapons also focused on the first, completed the scene.

"Mortog's goons have been disarmed." Ty said, helping her up for a second time. "Your GTO must have shown up."

She looked into his gray eyes, disbelief giving way to euphoria. "We made it."

Chapter 17

Ria wouldn't let go of Ty's hand. She still couldn't quite believe they'd survived. The dreams had been so real, and the ending had never varied. They stood with the rest of the EPs in the office of the planetary ruler. Supreme Commander Torril Anantha sat behind the behemoth desk and signed an order of temporary planet-wide control. He established a joint leadership between Warder Zar and the young Zander Salvator. Curzans and Mitans would work together to form a new world order on Mitah. One where Curzans were free and equal. It wouldn't be easy, but it was a start.

Mortog was dead, President Gordat Prayda was locked up back on Sandaria, and things were starting to look up.

The healers had done their work and Rucon looked perfectly fine. His clothes, however, told another story. Prayda had crossed a line that could never be undone. For the time being his containment on Sandaria would do. There were much larger issues for the commander of the GTO to deal with. Upheavals similar to Mitah were erupting across the galaxy with the fall of the empire, and the GTO had only so many resources. Then there were the Portal Masters complicating the situation on Sandaria. In Ria's opinion, arrest was too good for Prayda. If she ever found herself near him again, he would regret it.

Ria turned to Ty. *"You sure about this?"*

After Mortog's death and living through the dream, Ty had found a peace. Ria had felt it descend over them like a warm blanket. The driving force that had guided him since his parents' death was fading. In its place were their bond and a universe to explore.

"I killed the acting PR. Even with Anantha's pardon, too many Mitans want to see me dead. I can visit with the portal. Secretly." He cast a glance

out the windows to the city of Starfall beyond. *"I'm looking forward to seeing other worlds. And getting to know my mate properly without fearing for our lives."*

Ria winked at him. *"Now there's a concept. You're going to love my villa. Our villa. It overlooks an amazing lake in a country called Italy."*

Rucon brought their attention back to the group gathered before them. "We're ready."

A vid feed of young Zander Salvator projected from Rucon's com. He stood with rapt attention.

Rucon introduced everyone and brought him up to speed on what had transpired.

Zander stood dumbfounded a few moments before finding his voice. "This is extraordinary. I can't believe how things have changed overnight. I never liked Mortog, but there was nothing I could do until I came of age."

"Consider yourself of age," Commander Anantha said.

Rucon smiled at that. "There's one more thing you need to know."

Everyone waited while Rucon seemed to gather his thoughts. "Before Mortog took me captive, I discovered he was attempting to control my mind, my thoughts."

"Is that even possible?" Ria asked.

"It's extremely rare," Rucon said. "I had the healers do some research. The ability manifests itself in different ways and has different side affects depending upon who's using the power. With Mortog dead, we can't do any testing, but your healers are fairly certain he was exerting control over your parents. They report a change in both of their demeanors already. They don't know the extent to which they may recover, but you should come home as soon as possible. I'm sure you can arrange to finish your studies remotely. You and Warder have a lot of work to do, and you may get your parents back."

Ria could only imagine the range of emotions the poor guy must be going through.

Anantha stood and gathered up his things. "Good luck, Zander. I hope your parents make a full recovery. We'll expect you here within the week. Warder Zar will be setting up office down the hall. The numbers of underground Curzan are staggering. Equalizing the housing situation and getting them assimilated is going to take time. The Mitan population needs you here. They need to see your support of Warder and need to understand the transition ahead."

Warder crossed his arms. "I look forward to working with you, Zander."

"And I, you," Zander said. He let out a deep breath. "I have much to do. I will let you know my arrival date. In the meantime, I think we should make a joint announcement…" He paused.

Warder smiled. "Call me as soon as you can. We'll work together to determine exactly what we're going to say."

"That should make for some interesting viewing," Ian said. He turned to his team. "Ready to go home?"

They all agreed.

Ria squeezed Ty's hand and finally let go. "We'll get Ty's things loaded on the transport ship and port over later."

* * * *

Ty sat outside and soaked up the sun on his new home planet. He liked Earth, or at least what he'd seen of it so far. Ria was in town with one of her support agents, Gina, to pick up some last minute items for the Cavacents' gathering later. Although tempted to go, he'd opted to stay here and get in another workout in the sim room. He was still in awe of that space. Entire worlds fabricated out of thin air. Armond had tried to explain the physics to him, but manipulating quantum structures wasn't his forte. He was improving but had a long way to go. After being killed by multiple alien life forms for the third time in two hours, he'd needed a break.

His com buzzed. He glanced down to see that Dani and Ian had arrived. "Out here," Ty called. Strictly speaking, since he was training to become an Earth Protector, Ian was his new boss. But the Cavacent clan were a tight knit group that felt more like family. He stood to greet them.

"Where's your betrothed?" Dani asked.

"She's in town with Gina. Should be back any time."

"Slacking off?" Ian asked.

"Pfft. I just finished two hours in the sim room. Still getting my ass kicked."

Dani gave his arm a squeeze. "Ria said you're getting better."

His skill was improving every day, and it felt good. "Ria's a brutal task master. Or mistress."

"I know what you mean," Dani said. "She trained me on Sandaria."

Ian glanced around and clasped his hands together. "Looks like it's self-serve. Vino, love?" he asked Dani.

"Sure."

Ian left to procure drinks, and he and Dani sat to enjoy the last of the day's sun.

"Ria told me about you," Ty said. "It must have been pretty wild to discover you had psi. And escaping Gordat Prayda like that. You guys aren't short on adventures."

"It's been nonstop since the day Ian healed me and discovered my psi." She turned and studied his face.

"What?" he asked.

"You. You look more relaxed than I've ever seen you before. Clearly, this life suits you."

He inhaled deeply and nodded, taking in the view of the lake below. "I spent most of my life carrying around a lot of anger. You know about my parents?"

"Yes."

"It's like I'm finally making peace with all that. Their killer is dead, and the Curzans on Mitah are free. I only wish my parents were around to see it all."

"I'm glad you're at peace." She paused and leaned forward. "Did Ria tell you about my parents?"

He shook his head.

She toyed with a thread on her shorts. "They were killed in a plane crash when I was fifteen. That's when I went to live with my aunt on Cat Island." She met his gaze then. "My parents weren't brutally murdered, but I know what it's like to miss them everyday."

Ty reached out and pulled her into a hug. "Thanks for sharing that."

"You're welcome. Ria's like the sister I never had, which makes you something like a brother-in-law."

"I'm not gone ten minutes and you're already hitting on my psi-mate?" Ian joined them and handed Dani her drink.

"I just told him about my parents," Dani said.

"Ah." Ian kissed her gently on the lips. "It's an unfortunate thing to have in common."

"Time to lighten the mood," Ty said standing. "I'm going to go clean up. I'll see you in a few."

* * * *

Ria got home to find Dani and Ian enjoying the veranda. Saying her hellos, she ran upstairs to hang up a shirt she'd purchased in Como. She heard the shower running in the bathroom and smiled. Her psi-mate. She was still amazed at having found him. If they hadn't gone to the Summer's

Ball on Mitah… She couldn't go there. The thought nearly sparked a panic attack. She locked the door, took off her clothes, and entered the bathroom just as he was stepping out.

His hair hung over one eye, and he threw her that sexy-ass grin that made her heart melt and her body hum.

"You realize we have company," he said, wrapping his arms around her.

"They can wait."

The impossible buzz that only psi-mates could experience took over the moment he took her in his arms.

The kiss had a gentleness that stunned. She responded in kind, searching and exploring his lips and tongue. He tasted faintly minty. She nibbled his lower lip and breathed him in. He ran his tongue along her jaw finding a spot just below her ear that sent shivers all over. Their psi danced an equally tender duet.

Music came on, a male voice and a beat that made them sway.

"Nice touch." Ria slid her hands up his back and weaved her fingers threw his black hair. He moaned as she ran her nails along his scalp.

Their bodies had a language all their own. She visited every place she'd found that pleased him. Bringing her hands forward and down over his chest. She took half a step back and took him in from head to toe. He was so fracking beautiful. She kept her fingertips on his chest, holding him at arm's length. He was all muscle. Perfectly sculpted thighs and a narrow waist, not much larger than her own. As usual, his black hair half covered his face. She brushed it aside and marveled at the gray lights glowing in his eyes. She sighed as she dropped her hands and stepped closer. The heat inside was starting to burn, and their psi pulsed faster, moving them into a quicker tempo.

He found the spot behind her ear and trailed his teeth down her neck. Gripping her hips, he rubbed his cock against her clit. She threw her head back, and he bit her neck, sending a thrill through her. Pleasure washed over her, and their psi merged, causing a euphoria that only psi could.

Ty let out a moan of his own and pushed her up against the wall. He captured her mouth with a growing urgency. Reaching down, he lifted her leg up to his hip. He held her pinned as he slid his hand between her legs and guided himself inside.

Ty gave her what she needed with every thrust. The feel of him gliding into her was pure heaven. Ria bit down on his shoulder as he pumped. *Oh, Gods.* Each plunge brought her impossibly higher as their psi matched the intensity. Faster and faster. She cried out as the orgasm took her over the edge. Ty pumped harder a few more times before joining her in pure bliss. The world was green and gray.

Their breathing slowed, and the beating of his heart danced on her chest as he pressed a kiss on her neck, lingering, licking, so intimate. Returning fully to their bodies, he wound his fingers through her hair and used his thumb to tilt her face up to meet his.

"I beg your pardon, madam." Harvey's muffled voice came from her jean's pocket in the other room.

"What is it?" Ria called out.

"Miss Dani is downstairs and was wondering if you'd perhaps gotten lost."

Ria laughed. "It's good to have you back, Harvey. Tell her we're on our way."

"As you wish, madam."

"We should get going," Ty said, but still he held her pinned to the wall.

"We should." She moved her hip ever so slightly. "To be continued later?"

He moaned and ground into her before letting go of her leg and stepping back. They could both go again here and now, but he was right. She gave him a quick kiss before going to fetch her clothes.

* * * *

Ty kept a hand on the small of Ria's back as they descended the stairs. He was half tempted to turn her around and take her again, but they were already late to their own dinner. Downstairs, the gathering was heating up. Rucon and Mara stood near the bar, and Ian's Earth Support Agent, Jared, had just arrived. Armond and Marco stood talking to Ian's uncle Mordo and his companion Durgan.

Ty waved at Battista and Gina. The older Italian couple were Ria's support agents, and therefore his, and lived with them at the villa in a spacious guest suite off the kitchen. They were setting out appetizers and plates for the evening. Music played, and the doors were open to the patio outside.

Balastar was the last to arrive, having obviously come straight from his transport ship. Ty hadn't expected to like the ex-councilmember. He'd assumed all the emperor's council were corrupt, but had since learned that wasn't the case. Balastar's father had lost his life trying to stand up to the former emperor, and he wasn't shy about sharing his hatred of the previous regime. That scored him points. He also had a sarcastic sense of humor that Ty enjoyed. He and Ria headed over to say their hellos.

"You're looking more and more like a space pirate every day." Ty clasped him on the shoulder.

"In another lifetime maybe," Balastar said. "I'll stick to the right side of the law for now. Mostly."

Ria gave him a brief hug, and they joined the rest of the party.

Mordo and Durgan were in a heated discussion with Armond, causing everyone to gather around.

"That would be the implication," Armond said.

"What's up?" Ria asked.

"Armond has made an interesting discovery with the portal devices," Mordo said. "Go ahead and fill them in."

Armond was happy to oblige. "I've been working with Dani and Ian, teaching them how to use the device. With the assistance of myself and the other Portal Masters, they can both now create portals between two of these devices."

"That is so cool," Ria said.

"Indeed," Armond said in his usual haughty tone.

Ria stuck her tongue out at him, and he continued.

"It would appear we were correct in our assumption that these devices use an alternate form of psi. One that everyone capable of using the device shares. In further narrowing the implications, we have discovered that those who have Sandarian blood can use just one of these devices and anchor to an existing portal. That is how I was able to rescue Dani and Ria and send Rucon directly to Earth when we fled Sandaria. At the time, I was unaware that I was doing anything unusual. Mara, myself, and Dani all share the alternate form of psi, but because Dani is not Sandarian, she is unable to anchor to anything other than another one of these devices."

"I'm not complaining," Dani said, throwing her hands up. "The fact I can create a portal at all blows my mind."

"And we still have no idea where that alternate psi comes from?" Rucon asked.

"Correct."

"Balastar has agreed to help us continue the search," Mordo said.

Balastar nodded. "I've got a shipment heading back to Florin 5 where we found the other device. I'll track down the vendor and see if I can find out where he got it."

Rucon nodded agreement, then raised his glass. "A toast. To a successful mission, the freedom of the Curzans, and an ungodly number of upcoming weddings."

Laughter filled the night and glasses clinked. The rest of the evening flowed with laughter and wine. It was a domestic bliss Ty never expected. When the last guest was gone, he pulled Ria close and gazed into her green eyes. He traced her lips with his thumb. This amazing creature had brought him peace for the first time since he was a boy. And love. Never had he been as happy as he was with this woman in his arms.

Meet the Author

Sabine is a life long fan of Science Fiction and Romance novels. When the Alien Attachments series gelled in her imagination, she knew she had to share the world. Sabine lives in Florida with her husband, kids, cats and a whole mess of characters in her head.

www.SabinePriestley.com

Preview

Be sure not to miss Sabine Priestley's first book in the series!

Finding one's psi-mate is something every Sandarian hopes for, but when Ian Cavacent accidentally starts the bonding process with the Earthling, Dani, he has to fight his desire with every ounce of his being. If the process is completed, it would be both political and financial suicide for Ian and his family.

A natural klutz, Dani somehow always manages to land on her feet and win her mixed martial arts matches. At home on Cat Island, her balance is thrown when bazillionaire Ian takes notice. Unfortunately some butt-ugly Torog aliens also take notice, sending her life spiraling out of control and into Ian's arms. But Dani isn't the type of woman to let alien voodoo decide her future or her mate…no matter how gorgeous the man is or how much pleasure he gives her.

For centuries the Cavacents have mined Earth for a precious element, carnium, while protecting the planet from other alien species. Thanks to the Torogs, Dani and Ian must flee to Sandaria. As Dani learns to use her newfound psi powers, the empire crumbles around them.

Will their love be strong enough to keep them alive and get them back to Earth?

Chapter 1

A dark-skinned male and a tall blond female danced around each other, bamboo sticks at the ready, waiting for an opening. Sitting on the warm iron bleachers above, Ian Cavacent leaned forward in anticipation. The old warehouse on Cat Island doubled as many things. Tonight, it hosted the weekly mixed fight competition. The popular event drew crowds from as far away as Nassau. Humans jostled for a seat or stood in groups around the improvised, oversized boxing ring. The target of his interest was the blond woman. He'd come to watch her for the past few weeks. A friend of his human support agent, Jared, she fascinated him. He had a rule to avoid women on the island, but there was something about this one. She intrigued him. And not for the usual reasons, either. Yes, she was pretty, beautiful even, but there was more to it than that.

Jared slid into the seat next to him and handed him a beer. "Dani said you were stalking her."

"I don't stalk." Ian took the plastic cup. "Besides, I wasn't aware she knew I was here."

"Yeah, she told me that too."

Ian took a long pull on the beer. "There's just something odd about her. Maybe it's the way she moves. Her motions aren't practiced, she's constantly off balance, and yet she pulls in win after win. If I didn't know better, I'd say the fights were rigged."

The crowd quieted, and tension rose as the timer ticked down to zero.

Below, the two continued their dance, circling each other. The man lunged and Dani twirled with an awkward step, but still managed to dodge the swing of the bamboo. Sweat dripped into the cleavage of her sports bra and down the small of her back, leaving a dark stain in the fabric. She parried left and right. As usual, her maneuvers were halting and lacked grace.

Ian winced when Jared erupted in one of his booming sneezes. Dani shot an annoyed glance their way. Big mistake. In that fraction of a second, her opponent swung his bamboo. The jagged tip grazed the skin below her left eye before slamming into her wrist. The impact pushed her over the edge. She ducked, nearly fell over, spun around and in a surprisingly fluid movement, sent her opponent's stick flying. The crowd erupted with cheers and jeers for both sides. Money changed hands and the tension evaporated. The two opponents approached each other. Cradling her wrist, Dani declined a handshake. They shared some good-natured words before they left the floor.

Ian's powerful psi allowed him to see a purple mist radiating from her injuries. "That's going to hurt," Ian said.

"Dammit," Jared mumbled, grabbing one of his ever-present tissues. "Can you tell how bad it is?"

"Not yet."

"Well"—Ian swallowed the dregs of his beer—"she may have won, but she's going to be out of commission for awhile. She's not going to be happy with you."

"Yep." Jared wiped his nose. "I best go down and apologize. Come with me? She knows you've been watching. Be kind of weird at this point not to say hello."

A wave of anticipation washed over him. Aside from his three support agents, he limited his involvement with humans to the occasional short-lived affair off the island. Yet his reaction to spending time with this woman surprised him.

"You know I prefer to keep my involvement with humans away from here." Still, he was tempted. On the verge of changing his mind, he sensed a pending communication. "Hold on, incoming message from Marco." Marco was the Earth Protector, or EP, currently on duty. He waited a beat for it to arrive.

We got company, boss. His com relayed the message.

"Apologies are going to have to wait. Someone's paying Earth a visit." Ian said.

Jared followed him out the back door.

* * * *

Dani wiped the sweat from her brow and followed Dugo out of the fight area. Bazillionaire Ian Cavacent and her friend Jared were leaving out the back. Ian always kept to himself, and as far as she knew, never fraternized with the locals except Jared. His recent interest in her sparked an explosion of fantasies. Even better, he seemed the type who would be okay with a "nothing complicated" scenario. And he was hot. Seriously hot, hence the fantasies. She'd love to get him in front of her camera…and a few other places. Those wavy blond locks and smoky green eyes. *Yum. Why haven't you contacted me, Mr. Cavacent?*

Dugo interrupted her musings. "Someone needs to tell Jared to take his allergy meds." He nodded toward her arm. "You okay?"

"I'll be fine." She gave him a good-natured nudge with her other elbow. "You almost got me there."

He took a hand towel off the supplies table and handed it to her. "You're bleeding."

The medic came over and applied antibiotic ointment and a butterfly bandage to her cheek. "You should have that looked at."

"I will," Dani said.

Dugo tossed the towel in the laundry bin. "Glad I missed your eye. Seriously, man. I didn't see you comin'."

"And that's the way it's done," Dani said with all the swagger she could muster. Which was a lot, even with the pain radiating from her wrist.

Dugo laughed. "So what do you say? Have a drink with me?"

"Dugo…"

"Hey," he said, shrugging. "I never see you with no one here. You fly around the world and take your pictures, but this is home. Why you not date anyone?"

"Who says I don't?" Dani could tell by his stance he wasn't buying it. Didn't matter, he didn't have to. It was her business. "Gotta go. Catch ya next time."